Finding Poe

A Tale of Inspiration and Horror

Finding Poe
A Tale of Inspiration and Horror

Leigh M. Lane

Cerebral Books
Henderson, NV

Special thanks to Dana Fredsti, Penny Cawthon, Tommy Lane, Lori R. Lopez, and the muses.

Chapter One

I woke to the sound of beating drums, their rhythmic pulse buzzing through me as though a spectral parade passed through my room. My still-sleeping mind had taken me to the curb of a shadowy street, and I watched some sort of dark, midnight carnival, with horned men marching by, leading before the heavy cart that carried their tarred and feathered main event. The horses that pulled it seemed unnaturally large, their hooves being nearly the size of saucers and their heads towering over the rest of the precession.

The man in the cart was unrecognizable, the sludgy tar and white chicken feathers covering his body obscuring his features. As the parade dragged him past me, I saw that one of the man's eyes had been tarred shut and the other was not an eye at all, but a giant glass marble that peered aimlessly all around as he writhed and screamed. The drums grew louder, and I felt their heavy beats synchronize with my pounding heart.

Finding Poe

When I came to, I could still hear the drums as though I had brought my nightmare back with me into the waking world. For a terrifying moment, I felt that I had summoned Death himself to my side. My heart beat furiously with the drums, stealing my breath. It was a terrible sensation, as if I might gasp my last lungful of air at any moment. Then, suddenly, I realized there were no drums, only the rhythmic beat of the train thundering down the tracks. I looked around the cramped cabin, working to steady my nerves as I reminded myself where I was.

I had bought a train ticket to Baltimore, but no one had asked me for it when I boarded the soot-stained railcar. I had claimed my seat then spent some time reflecting upon my decision to seek out this strange man, whoever he was. My husband had left behind a sealed envelope with his name on it, with instructions that it be hand-delivered in his absence. Although we had been on bad terms when he had passed, I still felt obligated to him.

I now watched as the noisy train moved slowly through unknown territory. It was just on the brink of dusk, so perhaps that's why the surrounding flats of farmland looked so ominous. A light rain distorted my view of the outside, the falling streaks separating the terrain in strange, jagged breaks, but still I stared out, watching as we continued onward toward my destination. Flashes of the past several months broke my concentration, and I slipped into reverie as I continued to stare out the hazy, water-streaked window.

* * * *

Brantley had desperately wanted to go to the lighthouse. How he had learned about the situation, I do not know, but when I had discovered his insane plan, I had done my best to put an end to it. He had tried to use his title to gain access to the American appointment, one that was so far beneath us both that at first I had thought it a jest. Why he had suddenly felt the need to move us across the ocean to a remote rock off the coast of New England had been beyond me, but I had more influence than he—or so I had thought. His mother had been a widowed baroness, and although he had owned land, the Instrument of Government had left him no claim to a title by lineage. I, however, have always been a Lady, a twice-removed cousin of Frederick, Duke of Saxe-Lauenburg. How Brantley had managed to work his favor over mine is still a disturbing enigma, but perhaps sometimes not even the influence of a distinguished Lady can alter the course set by some Fates.

I should have seen the signs of Brantley's madness from the beginning, but for some reason I had not detected it until it was too late. I'm not certain how he was able to deceive me for so long, but I presume if he could fool his contacts into believing that he was the twice-removed cousin of my own—as if he might put the nobility to better use—he was capable of convincing anyone of anything. Perhaps my love for him had jaded my thoughts. I suppose it doesn't matter now. He accepted that awful position, despite all my efforts to stop him, so I had no choice but to take my leave alongside him.

Our voyage from Norland to New England was

hellish, Brantley's violent seasickness and my regrets over the move creating much misery between the two of us. We had been newlyweds still when he had begun to obsess over not just any lighthouse, but the Burnswatch lighthouse in New England. He had tried to convince me that some secret truth was hidden there, that a wise and trustworthy friend had confided it to him. He warned me that our life would have to become much simpler for a while, but nothing could have prepared me for the sudden and drastic changes that came with our move. No longer would we be hosting large parties or going with family and friends to the theater and the symphonies. No longer would we be attending functions or accepting invitations to elaborate balls. No longer would I have my housekeepers or my cook. A member of nobility living in a lighthouse was laughable, but a Lord and his Lady living in a lighthouse in New England were undoubtedly fleeing a scandal of some kind. It was mortifying, but it was also true.

When we neared our destination, I realized that the lighthouse was on a small island about a half mile offshore. When I inquired about the location, Brantley informed me that there were underwater hazards between the lighthouse and shoreline, and that unseen rocks and debris could damage larger ships if the lighthouse were not there to steer them away. I felt isolated just looking at it, and I could not help but protest as he ushered me to a wooden rowboat. When Brantley threatened to leave me at the dock, I knew he was serious, and I watched in silence as he slowly rowed us away from the mainland and toward our dark and secluded new home.

The lighthouse was cramped, and the tall spiral of stairs between the lantern room and the ground floor door made me feel uneasy. Our living quarters, a compartment on the ground floor that also held the maintenance closets, was damp and mildewed, and the sound of the waves crashing against the exterior was like an endless barrage of giant hands beating at the tower's base. The place smelled of mold and lantern oil, which had an odor that I might only describe as similar, but not quite the same, as rotting tallow. I told Brantley that the place felt unsafe, that the foundation had looked unsteady, the masonry old and worn, and I feared we would topple into the ocean at any time.

"Don't be silly!" he scoffed, a strangely angry hint to his tone.

"Did you get a good look at the base outside?" I asked him. "I could swear it's made of chalk!"

He crossed his arms. "The base is fine."

"And what about the mildew?"

He looked around. "We're in a *lighthouse*."

"Still, it can't be safe to live in such damp conditions," I said. "Have you thought about the dinner parties we will no longer be suited to host? And what about the prospect of starting a family? We absolutely could not raise a child here, Brantley!"

"I don't see you with child," he replied, his voice even and his eyes cold.

I turned away, unable to bear looking at him—at those eyes—any longer.

The silence between the two of us held through the night, and we went to bed with our backs to one another. No kiss. No loving touches. Just silence.

The dark room was cold, and I could see part of the spiral that led up to the lantern room from where I lay. I watched the flicker of light that reflected its way down the spiral, ending just at the edge of my range of view. The light waxed and waned like my own private blanket of moonlight, the spinning lantern seeming to power something even greater than its beacon to the sea. It seemed to give the place a life of its own, and something told me it didn't want me there. Perhaps it was just the strange draft that the lamp's heat sent to the exhaust hole at the top of the tower, the resulting upward rush of air through the spiral staircase creating a ceaseless hum that was both breathtaking and terrible.

It took me a long time to fall asleep. I would try to close my eyes, but either the haunting hum of the air or the ever-shifting light would call them open again. I considered rolling over.

I dared not do that, lest Brantley assume I was no longer as angry as he was.

With that horrific sound and the light spinning overhead . . . growing, then shrinking, then growing again . . . how could I help but open my eyes each time I sought to keep them shut? Still, I craved sleep, and I was determined that I would win my battle over insomnia.

I closed my eyes . . . again, and again, and again; however, sleep did eventually find me, as little relief as it gave me.

"Help me!" cried a little boy as I moved through a dense forest. Tall evergreens towered overhead and distorted the ground with their thick root systems. Patches of sunlight peeked through the erratic canopy, but the air was cold and I could see my breath as I hurried toward the source of the cry.

I slowed as I neared an old, half-dead tree. The trunk was enormous, but it roots seemed determined to hold their tight grip into the earth, despite the cavernous passage that spanned through the bulk of the rotting base. I peeked in, but the boy did not seem to notice me. He huddled, shaking, in the heart of the rotting grotto. He was around five years old, with short, blond hair and a lanky build.

"Hello," I said.

He gasped with a start as his eyes, wide and terrified, made a quick, vigilant turn toward me.

"Did you call for help?" I asked.

He stared at me, his mouth gaping open to respond, but falling silent.

"What are you doing out here all by yourself?"

His demeanor suddenly changed, the fear etched across his face transformed in an instant to a perplexing fusion of curiosity and defiance. "I could ask the same of you."

I felt the urge to gasp, the words seeming atypical for a boy his age. What did I know, though? I was no mother. I did not know the first thing about children.

"What's your name?" he asked.

I gave him a humble bow. "I am the Lady Karina of Norland."

"The Lady Karina?"

I nodded. "Who are you?"

He looked down.

"Are your parents nearby?" I asked him. "Perhaps I could help you find them." When the boy didn't respond, I knelt to peek in at a better angle, and I assessed the cave-like structure made by the old roots and rotting base. Although the interior was less than five feet tall, it was large enough for at least three or four full-grown men to duck inside without overcrowding one another.

"Why don't you come out of there?" I asked the boy. "We can search together."

"Why don't you come in?" he asked back.

I thought about all of the spiders, termites, and rodents that potentially used that dark, hollowed trunk as their home, and I shied back with a suppressed shiver.

The boy perked up. He got to his feet. "What's wrong? Are you afraid that maybe the tree trolls will get you?"

I shook my head. "I've never heard of tree trolls."

"Oh," he said, still standing there. "You have nothing to be afraid of then."

I stayed where I was. Something made my heart race and my palms go sticky with sweat. Something told me to stay back, to get some distance between me and the tiny passage. Something told me it was time to run.

I didn't run, though. I couldn't leave that little boy in there.

"Are you afraid of tight places?" he asked.

"No, not that it's any of your concern."

"You look a lot like someone I know who's afraid of all manner of tight places," he said.

I shrugged, my instincts still screaming at me to

run far away from there. "Whomever you know, it's not me. Come on out, and I'll help you find your parents."

He shook his head. "First, you have to come in here. It's actually very cozy. I like it in here. Do you think someone could live in a place like this?"

I trembled at the sudden thought of the lighthouse and the similarities it held to the tall tree's tiny cavern. I imagined the light, that endlessly spinning light, and I began to hear the hum of its haunting wind tunnel.

The boy offered me a wicked smile. "This could make a nice home, don't you think?"

"I can think of all kinds of vermin that could live here quite comfortably," I said. "Come out before you get bitten by a rat."

"A rat?" he asked, cocking his head. "In here?"

"Yes, a rat."

"No," he said, shaking his head again. "There are no rats in here. Nor are there any spiders or other creeping things."

I took another step back, keeping the boy just within eye contact.

"What's wrong?" he asked. "Is it something I said?"

I shook my head, although there was something very much wrong. I hadn't told him about my fear of the various types of vermin that potentially lived down there, and yet he listed the ones on the forefront of my mind. I told him as I took another step back, "I'm not going in there, so if you want my help, you'll have to come out."

The boy scoffed.

"I'm leaving now, so you can either join me or stay there. It's your choice," I said as I turned to walk away.

"Is it?" an unfamiliar voice said through the child's lips. The voice was deep and angry, like nothing I had ever heard come from a person, let alone a small boy. It stopped me in my tracks. I turned around and took a few steps back toward the tree, despite the loathsome feel it sent through the depths of my being. My entire body trembled. My stomach went tight. My chest became heavy, my heart pounding and my lungs laboring to draw in another breath of air.

"Which one of us would you save?" the thing speaking through the boy asked. "Man or monster? Child or fiend? Or might you risk your life for both?"

I watched as a red, luminescent glow surrounded him. His stare shifted from me to straight ahead, a dazed look flattening his affect. The red glow rose from his body and funneled into the tree. The red glow emanated around the tree for a moment, spinning like a lighthouse lantern, then disappeared.

The little boy looked around. "Where am I?" he whimpered, and then suddenly called out, "Help me! Somebody, please!"

Moved by the plea, I thought to reach for him, but I jumped back with a startled cry as the tree attempted to pull me in. I watched in horror as the opening transformed into jaws, the floor beneath the tree becoming a tongue, and the monstrosity began to chew the screaming boy. He made the most unspeakable of noises, screeching and moaning—then going deathly silent—as the tree ground him into meat and his blood flooded into the soil. I cringed back as it savored and chewed the boy's body like a person might the last bite of fine steak, and then it swallowed him with a muffled ripple up its tall, thick trunk.

I stood, my knees shaking, holding my stomach with both arms. I felt too weak to run, but the sight of the creature—and the possibility that it could be mobile—pushed me to turn and stumble away as quickly as I could.

I summoned the energy to run, putting a good amount of distance between the cursed tree and me before I allowed myself to slow my gait. I finally stopped in a clearing that looked empty, my body ready to collapse. I prayed nothing else would spring into view or transform with that same evil, translucent glow, as my need for rest was dire. I sat down in the center of the clearing, watching for any signs of change within view, then I fell to my hands and knees and began to vomit.

A strange sound, one I had heard before but still could not specifically place, began to emanate through the forest. I looked as far as I could through the trees, but I saw nothing. Try as I might to calm my nerves, I could not stop shaking. I heard the sound of a clock pendulum swinging from somewhere in the forest.

I looked up as a murder of crows flew overhead, cawing chaotically.

Suddenly, my name echoed "Karina?"

I looked around, recognizing the voice. "Brantley? Where are you?"

"Karina, are you all right?" he called again, his

voice echoing through the forest.

"Where are you?" I called back.

"Right *here*!"

I woke to an abrupt shake to my shoulders. Brantley knelt beside me as I lay stiffly across our new makeshift bed by the sea, which was in reality nothing more than a wide cot layered with quilts and pillows hardly fit for a Lady. I glanced over, contemplating Brantley's face as I took a moment to orient myself.

"I think you were having a nightmare," he said.

I still labored to breathe, and I took a moment to calm myself. Yes . . . a nightmare. Nothing more.

I turned to Brantley, letting him take me into his strong arms.

"It must have been a bad one," he said, and I knew he was prompting me to share.

I never lied to him, except when it came to my nightmares. I'm not sure why, but I always kept those to myself. I took a deep breath, then told him, "I don't remember much of it. I just know it was quite frightening."

"You're with me now," he said, his voice soothing.

I let him hold me, trying to enjoy the feel of his arms around me, trying not to be stiff and distant despite my continued anger and the awful images of that little boy still reeling through my mind.

"Are you sure you're all right?" Brantley asked me.

I nodded, giving him my best smile. "I'm perfectly fine."

Chapter Two

I rose early that morning, long before sunrise. I searched through the dark for my slippers and housedress, and quietly left through the heavy floor-level door. My body felt lighter as I stepped out of the lighthouse and into the morning fog, and my mood followed suit, growing ever lighter the further I got from the moldy, rotting structure.

The waning moonlight sifted through the heavy fog, creating a strange glow that grew only stranger with the lighthouse light rotating through it. I listened for the waves as I made my way through the foggy darkness. The air was moist and fresh, and the rocky ground beneath me was wet from the fog. When suddenly I hit sand, I stepped out of my slippers and continued barefoot.

I could hear the waves crashing so loudly that I felt certain I would feel the cold water rush over my feet at any moment. The fog deceived me though, somehow amplifying the sound. After several more paces, I found myself stepping from damp, loose sand into wet, compact sand. Still, I could not see the waves.

I saw the rush of the tide just a moment before it hit my feet, and I jumped with the shock of the cold water and pulled up my skirt as it rushed over my ankles. The water was numbingly cold, and I stepped back a few paces. I looked around through the pools of darkness and light swimming through the fog, finding the lighthouse light spinning nearby, then turned back to the ocean. I looked down as the cold tide hit my feet once more. Seaweed bobbed over to me, wrapping around one foot as the tide fell back. I knelt to free my foot, surprised at how tangled the seaweed had become over the course of just a few seconds.

The tide came back in, and I fell back with a scream as a bloated, decomposing human head floated in with the rush of water. Long tangles of dark brown hair meshed with a mass of seaweed, and I kicked the seaweed from my foot and staggered back as I watched the water take it away again. I hurried back toward the spinning light, nearly too terrified to breathe. I couldn't find my slippers, so I ran as carefully as I could across the rocky ground beyond the beach. I cut my feet over a few poorly chosen steps, but luckily, my injuries were minor. I began to sob as I found the door.

Brantley still slept as I felt my way through the dark, to the bed. "Brantley, wake up!" I cried.

"What's wrong?" he mumbled.

I struggled to catch my breath, barely able to speak past a couple of words. "There was a head, a severed head in the water!" I managed to utter.

"You've had another nightmare," he said, with an annoyed tone of voice.

I crawled onto the bed, moving beside him. "This wasn't a nightmare. Look—I have sand on my feet."

He sprang up and slid me off the bed. "What are you doing getting sand on the bed?"

I felt a spray of sand fall over me as he shook out the top quilt. "I'm telling you that I saw a head—"

"If you saw anything, it was a jellyfish," he interrupted, his voice going from annoyed to angry. "What were you doing out on the beach?"

"I couldn't sleep, so I thought I'd take a walk."

"No more of that. The beach is not a safe place for you to be wandering alone in the dark," he said. "Understand?"

I sighed, sitting to wipe the sand from my feet, wishing I could come up with some malicious yet witty response. None came, so I removed the last of the sand and got back in bed.

He began to snore, and that, combined with the endless noise of the wind tunnel, was nearly more than I could take. I knew I had seen a head. The thought of it flashed intermittently through my mind's eye. I desperately wanted Brantley to confirm my find and take it to the proper authorities, but he seemed more intent on sleeping than listening to anything I had to say, so I lay there, staring through the darkness, listening to the howl of the spiral staircase and the roar of Brantley's snore, wiping away my tears as they came.

What else could I do?

I turned as yet another sound hit my ear. It was shrill and chilling, as if a mythical banshee had dropped in through the top of the lighthouse. I strained to look up the staircase, but I saw nothing new. The creature shrieked again and I considered waking Brantley, but I remained still, afraid to anger him any further.

I cringed as the creature sounded off yet again, but to my relief, it still did not seem to be coming any closer. I looked all around, just in case it was trying to sneak up on me, but still I saw nothing. I waited for it to sound off again, but beyond the wind and Brantley's snores, everything once again was quiet. I listened harder, but the only additional sound that came to me was that of the waves crashing against the shoreline.

I grew restless, my mind far too awake for my body to fall asleep again, but I dared not get up. I imagined specters in all directions, all of them waiting for me to wander through the dark and fall into their grasp. I reminded myself that there were no such things as ghosts, that the lighthouse was *old*, not haunted. I could not make myself believe it, though, not completely. My intuition told me that there was something unnatural up there, something unearthly and nefarious that had terrible plans for me and Brantley both. Something told me that I needed to get out while I still could. Still, I did not move.

I lay beside Brantley, too afraid to do anything else as I watched for the first hints of daybreak. While I waited, I tried to ignore all that had been distracting me, but I could not. My mind took in all of the sounds with a level of amplification that seemed spitefully self-destructive. I tried to keep my eyes closed, but they seemed intent on seeking out the light despite me. Despite my wish that the banshee would not sound off again, I listened intently for it. Why I felt so set on trying my own sanity, I cannot say, but it seemed to me that the lighthouse was trying Brantley in similar ways.

All that morning, he was preoccupied with a matter of which he refused to share. He moved frantically about the lighthouse, counting the steps, timing the spin of the lamp, measuring the foundation. He took notes, carrying the ink and pen with him as he fussed with his measurements. I tried my best to leave him to his work, occupying myself with menial tasks I had thought below me before we had first set sail from Norland. Only because my nanny had been so intent on teaching me did I know how to sew and make a cross-stitch, and I learned from the other emigrants onboard the ship how to boil and scrub my own laundry. I still had much to learn about preparing food, not that it mattered, given our limited provisions. We had a few different kinds of preserves, some dried corn, and a couple of cast iron pots, and I struggled to make use of them all.

In many ways, I cursed this new life—and I cursed Brantley for bringing me here. I had not a worry in the world back in Norland, at least not before Brantley had endured the transgressions of that insufferable peasant. He had deserved it for becoming so friendly with the help. I never would have stooped so low as to go drinking with the cook, or even with my retired childhood nanny, but Brantley had deemed it fully acceptable to get drunk with the footman. He had brought the scandal onto himself.

I often wondered if I would have been better off staying behind, despite everything, although I know I really had no choice but to go. We both had no real choice, although a lighthouse off the coast of New England was an extreme choice of retreat.

"I promise I'll be able to give you the life you deserve very soon," I remember him telling me while we watched the waves carrying us across the seemingly endless field of blue. "When I find what I'm looking for, this will all pay off."

"But why so far away from home?" I asked him.

A suspicious look came over him as he pulled me close. "It will all make sense when we get there. You have to trust me!"

But when we arrived, nothing made any more sense than it had, and if anything Brantley became even more secretive about his reason for choosing this specific lighthouse. The strange measurements and erratic trips up the lamp tower continued. He counted the stairs, the number of times it spiraled to the top, and how many times the lamp turned while he darted from the bottom to the top, then back down. He counted, and then recounted, every visible brick both inside and out.

Each time I would ask him about his work, he would insist simply that I trust him. One day, however, he greeted my question with the strangest request.

"Would you go to town for me?" he asked. "You'll have to take the rowboat, but we're not that far offshore."

"You want me to take a rowboat to the mainland?" I asked him, incredulous. "Why can't you go?"

"Because you're not trained in proper lighthouse emergency protocols!" he snapped. "We need supplies!"

I watched him for a moment, unsure how to respond. I tried to remain calm, despite the strange look he began to give me, a chilling, unexpected twitch momentarily contorting his sweaty, angry face. Suddenly, he didn't look anything like himself. It was as if he had transformed into some terrible, hateful creature that wanted nothing more than to get rid of me—one way or another.

Without daring to say another word, I agreed to go.

I had never personally worked a rowboat before, and even after Brantley had instructed me on its use, I had great difficulty negotiating it through the water. The morning fog had long burned off, the day was clear and the water calm, but still I could not manage to steer that tiny boat in a straight line. Luckily, a breaker just beyond the lighthouse kept the waves tame, so even though it took all morning for me to get across the short stretch, I had little fear of flooding or capsizing. Brantley had warned me to stay in the boat until I could clearly see the beach beneath the water, as masses of jagged rocks lined the shallow areas and wading even in waist-deep water was potentially hazardous.

I had no desire to get my dress wet, so I waited for the low, rolling tide to take me as far as it would onto the beach. I did my best to pull the boat onto higher land, as I saw nothing to tether it to, then I made sure I had my canteen and moneybag on me as I began to follow Brantley's instructions to town.

The beach slowly shifted to rocky grassland, then to rolling fields. By the time I reached the patch of forest Brantley had described as the last barrier between the ocean and the town, the day had lapsed to late afternoon. The forest's edge seemed unintimidating enough, but it wasn't long before I looked all around and became disoriented by the vast span of trees now surrounding me. I realized that I had lost track of my direction, and suddenly I felt like that little boy huddled in the mouth of an enormous monster, waiting for the jaws to emerge and eat me alive.

For a few minutes, I stood frozen in fear, unsure which way to continue. I tried to find the sun through the treetops, but I could not determine the direction from which it shone. Unsure how else to proceed other than choosing a direction and beginning to walk, I continued, thoughts of the impending sunset driving me forward. Already the forest was getting darker, a single shadow blanketing the trees. I knew that I only had a limited time before the last hints of sunlight left and the forest went from dark to pitch black.

The darkness descended quicker than I had anticipated, and soon I found myself stumbling from tree to tree, blinded by the darkness. I struggled to remain calm despite my helplessness, doing my best to keep moving. Crickets chirped and an owl stalked something nearby. I tried to ignore them, knowledge of their existence bringing about images of other larger creatures existing alongside them, creatures that might possibly be stalking me. I knew little about the local wildlife, but I imagined that the predators were many.

I turned as I noticed a light appear in the distance. At first, I thought someone had a campfire burning, but as I got closer, I realized that it was the glow of a fireplace through a cottage window. The scent of burning pine, then of stewed meat and onions, hit my nose, and for the first time that day, it occurred to me that I was hungry. I felt a nervous pang offset my hunger for a moment as I began up the path to the front door. When I reached it, I hesitated to knock, fearful of what might come of such an unexpected intrusion. As I stood silently considering my options, I did not notice the black cat approach from the darkness. I jumped back as it met me on the doorstep and rubbed against the skirt at my ankles.

The cat was large, clearly a tom, with a tiny patch of white fur that made him look as though he wore a baby's bib. What was most striking about the cat, however, was that he had a single yellow eye, with an empty socket in place of the other. He seemed unbothered by the partial blindness, happily seeking my attention as I continued to contemplate my next move.

The cat pawed at the door with an agitated mewl, and I considered sprinting off into the darkness as I heard a dog bark, followed by approaching footsteps. The door was open before I could move, and I stood stiffly as a tall man looked down at the cat running in between his feet, then over at me, his clumsy hound circling me. The man appeared to be in his late twenties or early thirties, with reddish-blond hair and a dark, red beard. The scent of the stew flooded out as he opened the door a little further, then the sudden stench of liquor hit me as the man opened his mouth to speak.

"Is it yours?" he asked in English, seemingly just as dazed by my presence as I was with his.

"What?" I asked, fearing that perhaps my incomplete grasp of English had added to the vagueness of his question.

"The cat. Is it yours?" he asked.

I shook my head. "He's not yours?"

"He can't possibly be mine!" the man said, his eyes going wide as he too shook his head. His face went white as his expression shifted to one of suspicion. "Who are you? What are you doing here?"

"Please forgive my intrusion. I have been wandering lost in these woods all night, and I saw the light from your fireplace."

He gave me a strange look of disbelief. "Lost?"

I nodded. "My husband sent me to town for supplies, but I'm afraid the directions he gave me were not very good."

"Town?" he asked.

A young woman came up behind him and placed a gentle hand on his shoulder. "Let the poor woman in, John." She urged the door completely open, offering me a sympathetic smile. "Please excuse my husband. He's had a trying week."

The young woman, Elizabeth, convinced her husband to let me stay the night, and she offered me a bowl of stew and a seat by the fire. The dog lay beside me, while the cat curled up against John's legs. He drank rum from a bottle, his discomfort over the cat's presence obvious.

The hound turned to me, his eyes begging for a bite of meat from my stew.

"You already had yours, Neptune!" Elizabeth said. "Leave the poor woman alone!"

John mumbled something, but I was unable to catch what he said.

"I cannot believe your husband turned you out alone in this wilderness," Elizabeth said. "Of all the cruel ways a man might rid himself of his wife—"

"He sent me to town for supplies. It's likely my own fault I got lost," I felt the need to tell her.

"Which town?" she asked.

I shrugged. "He didn't say."

"The closest town from here is a day's journey by horseback," she said. "He couldn't possibly have expected you to walk that far and back by yourself."

I set aside my stew, no longer hungry. The three of us sat in silence for some time, listening to the crackle of the fireplace and contemplating the strange evening. It was John, his face growing suspicious once more, who finally spoke.

"Where was it you said you lived?"

"My husband and I just moved to the lighthouse," I said, suddenly feeling the full weight of my new lowly social status.

John's face went even graver. "The *Burnswatch* lighthouse?"

I nodded.

I turned to Elizabeth, and she too now watched me with a confusing look of fear and contempt.

"Why?" she asked, shaking her head.

"I don't know why, but I'm very unhappy about the place," I said. "Brantley obviously was not in his right mind when—"

"Why did you have to curse us with you?" the woman shrieked.

I got to my feet, confused by the couple's alarm, afraid now that either might strike out at me over what obviously had to be some wild American folktale. "I don't understand!"

The cat raced back into the room, and to my surprise, the man kicked it as it passed him by. "You're *not* my Pluto!" he howled as the cat scrambled to its feet and scurried away.

I wondered if either would pursue me should I race for the front door, then the hound began to bark, guarding my moves, clearly aware of my alarm.

John pointed at me, his eyes wild with rum and superstitious angst. "He *is* your cat! Admit it!"

I stayed where I was, knowing I was cornered. "I don't know what you're talking about!"

"Admit it!" yelled the man.

"Harbinger of doom!" yelled his wife.

"No!" I cried, my breath escaping me as he went for an axe on the wall.

He turned to me with a crazed look, like nothing I had ever seen before, and I knew without a doubt that he meant to kill me. I ran despite the hound at my heels, and Elizabeth rushed in to stop me.

"It's the only way!" she cried, grabbing me by the sleeve.

John raised the axe over his head, taking aim at mine, but as he came down, the hound swept my legs and took me to the ground with Elizabeth coming down hard against me. The axe sank deep into her head, and I screamed as blood sprayed over us both.

The hound turned on his master at the grim sight, sinking his teeth into the man's leg as I scrambled to my feet.

I heard the dog's cry as the man struck it hard, then the sound of it hurrying behind me as I ran blindly into the dark forest. I ran into trees and stumbled over brush, cutting and bruising my body in my attempt to continue ever forward. I began to cry aloud, feeling certain the hound was intent on taking me down as well, but to my surprise, he howled mournfully at my side. I began to slow, my lungs burning and my heart racing, and the hound slowed with me. When finally I could run no longer, he too stopped to catch his breath.

I sat beneath a large evergreen, sweating in the cold, and the dog began to lick my face.

I sat back, sighing my relief as I realized I had outrun the danger. I petted the hound, which seemed eager to stay at my side. "I guess it's you and me now." I thought for a moment, ensuring I had remembered correctly his name. "Neptune?" I asked him.

He continued to lick my face, and then he stood back, tail wagging in the dim moonlight, as I got to my feet. Feeling empowered by my newfound companion, I continued through the forest on foot, slowly making my way through the darkness of the night.

Chapter Three

Despite my difficulties with both the darkness and the increasing cold, we continued without rest. I feared that the dog might abandon me should I stop for sleep, a risk I was unwilling to take. My body shivered, the cold inviting me to find a quiet spot beside a large tree and give in to my intense desire to huddle and sleep. Still, I continued, reaching into the black void, unsure of each step as I made it. I could not see Neptune at my side, but I could hear his steady gait. Every once in a while, his tail brushed against the thigh of my skirt, a more tangible assurance of one another's presence in which we both undoubtedly took some comfort.

I paused apprehensively as I heard something beyond the two of us. "Neptune, wait!" I ordered in a hushed whisper.

I listened carefully, unsure what the new sound was. It was rhythmic, but it definitely was not a drum. I stilled my breath, intent on identifying it, but the hound circled me restlessly, seemingly unwilling to stop moving. I tried to hush him as I noticed a light up ahead. My heart nearly leapt from my chest as I was able to identify the sound: it was that of spades hitting the hard earth. I considered the possibility that we had crossed into a cemetery and the men ahead might be grave robbers.

I moved to get a better look, moving a tree closer every time I summoned the courage. As I neared, I was able to see a small lamp hung on a low-hanging branch of an enormous tree and a second lamp on the ground nearby. Three men were hard at work, digging, but clearly (and much to my relief) they were not in a cemetery. This made their excavation all the more intriguing, and soon I stood close enough to hear the men exchanging small talk as they worked.

"This cannot be the right spot!" a portly Englishman said, taking a moment to rest against his shovel.

"I cannot be mistaken!" the second exclaimed in a New England accent and a heavy lisp. "My calculations were perfect!"

The third man, black skinned with hair that suggested African descent, continued shoveling, ignoring the other two.

"We've been at this all night!" yelled the Englishman. "Look at my suit!"

"It can't be much further down now!" snapped the New England man.

As I stood, silent and still, trying to decide what to do, Neptune thrust forward and exposed us with an apprehensive howl. The men stopped and turned to us all at once, and the Englishman screamed at the sight of the charging dog. Unable to abandon him, I ran behind him as quickly as I could. "Neptune!"

Neptune slowed as he reached the small pit, in which all three men still stood, dumbstruck by our presence. I clung to the trunk of a nearby tree as I tried to make sense of the strange scene.

"Why, hello, my dear," said the Englishman, dabbing his sweaty brow. "To what do we owe the honor?"

"I'm . . . Karina," I said, opting at the last moment to withhold my title. "I have been searching since morning for town, but I'm afraid my dog and I are lost."

"Town, you say?" asked the Englishman, an amused grin coming to his lips. "Where are you traveling from?"

"Near the coast," I told him, afraid to mention the lighthouse to anyone else, lest I experience a similar reaction to the last.

"You must be far down the coast," said the New England man. "This whole region is quite heavily populated."

"I see," I said, feeling even more confused than before.

The New England man moved to the side of their pit, and Neptune moved between us as he thought to climb out. "What are you *really* doing out here?"

"I told you, I'm lost," I said. "Would any of you be kind enough to point me in the direction of town, if it's so close?"

The men glanced amongst one another, looking unsure of what to do.

"What are *you* doing out here?" I asked, surprised by my own courage.

All three men seemed taken aback by my question, each nervously shifting foot, and it occurred to me that what I witnessed was indeed either illegal or secret. My breath nearly escaped me as I considered the possibility that they had been attempting to conceal a body when I came upon them. I glanced around, seeing nothing, and realized that it was not a grave they were digging. They were searching for something.

"What does it look like we're doing?" the New England man asked me.

I shrugged, struggling to think of something I might say to play at ignorance. "Are you clearing the land to build a cabin?" I asked, my voice shaky.

"Marvelous guess!" said the Englishman. "Why, we're digging the wine cellar right now!"

The New England man turned to his friend, then back at me with a nod and a smile. "Yes, a wine cellar."

I nodded back, hoping my smile didn't look too contrived. "So, if you could just direct me to town, I'll let you get back to your work."

The men looked amongst one another again, then the New England gestured to the black man. "Jupiter here would be happy to show you back to town. Wouldn't you, Jupiter?"

The man looked surprised, but eagerly set aside his shovel and climbed out of the hole.

"Take her to the inn, then come right back," said the New England man, handing over the second lantern.

My hound barked at the servant as he approached me.

"It's all right, Neptune," I said, petting the dog, and I acquiesced as Jupiter tugged on my sleeve and led me away from the pit. Neptune stayed obediently at my side.

We walked for several minutes in silence. I watched the lantern light as it shifted from tree to tree, illuminating only the ground immediately around us. It was a relief to be able to see where my feet were going, my body being sufficiently bruised and achy from the numerous trips and falls I had endured from my earlier wanderings through the dark.

"So, your name is Jupiter?" I finally asked him. "I've never met a man named Jupiter."

"My name is not Jupiter," he answered.

"So why do those men call you by it?"

He shrugged. "That's just what they call me."

"Why don't you correct them?"

He turned to me with a devilish smile. "They think I'm mute."

"Why would you play mute?" I asked.

"Why would you play stupid, woman?" he asked back. "We don't always get to choose our company, and mine is best kept ignorant of the fact that his servant is both educated and well spoken."

I thought for a moment, trying to make sense of the scenario.

"I'll gladly take being mute over uttering the broken English they ex*pect* me to speak," he added.

I nodded. "I see."

"You won't tell anyone, will you?"

I turned to him with a raised brow. "Tell me what those men were really digging for."

He looked around, as if to make sure no one else

was nearby, then said, "They think there's buried treasure out here—but I've seen the deductions my master's friend has made, and he's very clearly insane."

"Buried treasure?" I asked. "Out here?"

He nodded. "It all started when he heard about some clue hidden in a lighthouse, then he connected it to a golden brooch he had quite madly deemed alive for some time and—"

"A lighthouse?" I interrupted, surprised.

"The haunted lighthouse. Have you heard of it?"

I gave a nervous laugh. "Aren't all lighthouses haunted?"

He shook his head, giving me a suspicious eye.

"I don't care what they're doing out there," I said, "and I don't care that you're playing them both for fools. I just want to get to town, so I can figure out where I am and find my way back home."

He looked surprised. "So you really are lost?"

I nodded, heaving a relieved sigh as I saw the lights from the inn in the distance.

"You have an interesting accent. May I ask where you're from?" he asked.

"Norland."

"I can't say I've heard of it." He stopped, pointing to the lights. "I must go back now. Good luck to you in the rest of your travels."

I gave him a grateful nod. "Thank you." I watched him turn back down the dark, empty path, the light from his lamp waning as he moved into the distance.

"Let's go, Neptune," I told the dog, and together we continued toward town and to the inn.

Patrons filled the downstairs pub. I kept Neptune close to my side as I made my way to the barkeep.

The tall, big-handed barkeep had curly red hair and bright blue eyes. He filled a pint mug for a nearby man, then turned to me. I noticed that he was missing a front tooth as he smiled. "What can I do for you?" he asked.

"Whom do I speak to about a room?" I asked back.

"With the dog?" he asked.

"I'll pay extra," I said, allowing him a glimpse into my purse.

He moved to a locked cupboard, key ring in hand, and unlocked it. He grabbed one of only two available keys left, then quickly closed and locked the cupboard before turning back to me. "You're in luck. I have a loft where you should be very comfortable."

I nodded my thanks. "If you could show me to my room, I'd like to retire immediately."

I tried to bring Neptune with me as the innkeeper led me to the staircase.

"The dog stays downstairs," the man insisted.

"I promise he's a very clean dog," I tried.

The innkeeper shook his head. "He'll be fine by the fire, I'm sure."

I contemplated my situation, then finally conceded with a defeated nod. "Go lie down," I told Neptune, pointing to the fireplace.

The dog gave a tired huff and returned to his warm spot by the fire.

"This way," said the innkeeper, showing me upstairs.

The room was dark and quiet, but still I lay awake

for some time, reflecting upon the long day. When I did finally fall asleep, I awoke immediately to the sound of a loud crash downstairs and Neptune's loud, howling bark. I thought about going down there to see what had happened, but then decided against it in fear that the innkeeper might find some way to add even further charges to my bill. I listened carefully, noting a short commotion, and then once more all was quiet. I lay sleepless the rest of the night, too anxious about the possible damages to fall back asleep. I hurried downstairs in the early morning hours, before the innkeeper woke, cringed at the small mess of broken glass and overturned tables and chairs. I felt bad, but then reminded myself that the innkeeper had insisted on keeping Neptune downstairs. Refusing responsibility, I summoned the dog and quietly slipped out.

The town was disappointing in the predawn light, much smaller than I had anticipated. A helpful resident directed me to the market court, which turned out to be little more than a couple of fruit stands and a diminutive general store. I looked over the list Brantley had given me, surprised as I read it for the first time:

More grain and preserves,
A chicken (or eggs, if there are no chickens)
A goat (or cheese, if there are no goats)
A bottle of rum.

I glanced into my purse, wondering how much even the least on my list would cost. I had attended peasants to market back in Norland, but that was only to survey the fresh foods and find new flavors with which the cook might experiment. Shopping was an altogether new venture for me.

I found grain, but quickly realized that I would be capable of carrying very little of it. I also found eggs, a chicken, and cheese, but no goats. I bought a chicken, but it kicked away from me as I tried to carry it away and ran off. Neptune gave chase, but it won. I opted not to buy a second one. I spent nearly the last of my money on the bottle of rum, but as nearly empty-handed as I already was, I dared not return home without it.

When I asked one of the market hands how I might get back to the coast "near" the Burnswatch lighthouse, the little peasant woman informed me that we stood only an hour walk directly west from the lighthouse. I looked at my instructions and the convoluted journey Brantley had sent me on, and I decided to check with another resident for confirmation of the first's much simpler directions.

Indeed, we were due west of the Burnswatch lighthouse, the *haunted* lighthouse that now possessed my husband in some unspeakable way over some ridiculous, nonexistent treasure. I walked due east, supplies in hand and Neptune at my side, and together we reached the lighthouse by midday. I was relieved to find the rowboat was precisely where I had left it, although trepidation soon took hold as I thought about what awaited me once I boarded it. I coaxed Neptune to my side and summoned the strength to begin rowing us to the fog-patched island.

Chapter Four

Brantley uncorked the rum and took a heavy swig as soon as I handed it to him. He swallowed it with a grimace and took another. "What took you so long? I thought something terrible had become of you!" he yelled.

"*Your* directions sent me miles out of my way!" I yelled back.

"That's impossible! The directions I gave you were perfect!"

I crossed my arms, making a show of my protest with a loud scoff.

He swallowed another mouthful of rum. "You have no idea what you put me through!"

"You have no idea what I've *been* through!" I cried, summoning a heavy stream of tears. "No idea!"

He turned to Neptune, who now lay quietly at the base of the staircase. "I don't suppose it has anything to do with this dog you dragged in with you? How do you expect to feed it?"

"This dog saved my life, so I'll feed him my own dinners, if that's what it takes!"

He set down the bottle, his eyes already beginning to show his intoxication. He teetered just slightly as he took a step toward me. "It will disrupt my work!"

"Your work!" I looked around. "What work?"

He shook his head, clearly flustered. "I can't discuss it with you, not until I find what I'm looking for."

"Buried treasure?" I asked, raising a brow.

He froze, the color suddenly lost from his face. He blinked hard, turned to the rum bottle, thought better of it, and turned back to me with a heavy sigh. "Who told you about the treasure?" he finally asked.

I shook my head. "There is no treasure. It's all just a local legend."

He looked at me as though I had just slapped him. "Who told you that?"

My muscles went tight, something deep inside me telling me that I best find a way to calm him or flee. I rushed to Neptune's side, confident that he would protect me if my husband were to turn violent in his sudden drunken rage.

He stayed where he was, looking hurt and angry as he asked again, "Who told you that?"

"Does it really matter?"

"Yes, it matters!"

Neptune looked up at him, then at me, then set his head back down with an annoyed huff.

Feeling defeated, I shook my head and proceeded to relay to him my encounter with the three men in the forest. I told him every detail I could remember, including my private discussion with "Jupiter" the servant.

"And you believed him?" Brantley asked.

I nodded. "Why shouldn't I have?"

"Well, if he lied about being mute, wouldn't you suspect that he might be unreliable on other matters as well?"

I shrugged. "He lied about it for the sake of his dignity."

"That's ridiculous! Even if he did, obviously his loyalty still lies with his master."

"His master was on a nonexistent treasure hunt led by a mad Englishman!"

He shook his head incredulously. "*You* are mad!"

I suddenly realized that there was no convincing him of the deception. He was here to find buried treasure, and he wasn't going to abandon that illusion easily.

My words were meaningless to him.

"Believe what you want," I finally added, "but you have done wrong by me to move me here."

He gave me a hateful sideways glance. "Do you suggest we return to Norland?"

I looked down. "I'm not stupid."

"But apparently you think *I* am?"

I shook my head.

"Stupid enough to chase 'nonexistent treasure!'"

Lost for words, I continued to shake my head.

"I'll show you!" he roared, then moved past me to the staircase and ascended it. He clung to the railing as he rounded the helix, looking as though he might lose his balance and topple back down the steps. To my relief, he made his way to the top and disappeared into the lamp room.

I heard nothing from him for the next few hours save the sound of his footsteps as he frantically moved about upstairs. I busied myself with my needlework for a short while, as cross-stitch always seemed to calm me down, and then I paced the kitchen area as I labored to find something better than pancakes for supper. With great frustration, I surveyed the dirty kitchen. It seemed Brantley had attempted to cook for himself in my absence, the burned mess he left for me telling the tale of an attempt at pan-fried fish.

Fish?

I turned to the staircase. "Where did you get the fish?"

He gave no reply.

"Brantley?"

Nothing.

I moved to the foot of the stairs. "Brantley?"

Neptune jumped to his feet as I began to ascend the steps. I moved slowly, my chest growing tight as I approached the tower. I peeked in, finding Brantley standing nearby with his ear to the wall. I noticed the rum bottle remained roughly as full as it had been when he had retreated with it, and I was relieved to see that he appeared sober. Still, it seemed strange that he would be listening so intently to a wall.

He noticed me with a sudden glance and stormed over. "This had better be important! I'm in a foul mood!"

"I'm sorry—I was just wondering about the fish!" I said.

"What about the fish?"

"I was just wondering where you got it. I would

like to make fish and biscuits tonight for supper," I quickly decided, feeling tense and uneasy by his recent outbursts.

Strangely, his demeanor softened as he said, "When I was standing out on the shoreline last night, watching for you, I noticed an abundance of flounder."

"Why didn't you tell me this before?"

He shrugged.

"And you know how to catch them?" I asked.

He nodded.

"Could you catch some for supper?"

"I suppose I could," he said.

I gave him a thankful nod and turned to the staircase. "I'll just finish cleaning the kitchen then."

"You do that."

I had nearly completed one revolution down the steps when he peeked out. "Karina?"

I stopped and turned. "Yes?"

His features went strangely tight as he stared at me for a moment, then he said, "Come up here again, and I'll break both your legs. Do you understand?"

I fought to take a breath, a hot, heavy wave seemingly knocking me back against the railing. I nearly asked him to repeat himself, a part of me in disbelief that he would threaten me with such violence, but the look still etched across his face told me to leave without another word. I felt my throat go tight as I glanced down, no longer able to meet his hurtful stare. I gave him some semblance of a nod, and then turned and hurried down to the bottom of the staircase. Neptune was still standing beside the first step, looking apprehensive about moving up any further. I petted him as I reached the bottom and sat down on the first step, struggling to make sense of what had just occurred.

Neptune looked intently at me as I scratched his chin, as if he too sought an explanation.

"I think Brantley's just had a rough time of things," I said to the dog. "I think he's doing his best to cope with all he's been through."

Neptune cocked his head, as if to let me know he knew better. He followed me back into the kitchen, where I finished scrubbing the dishes. When I had all of the dishes sitting out to dry, I tossed out my dirty water and wiped down the sink. I found the broom and began sweeping what at first appeared to be sand and debris tracked in from the beach.

As I cleared the sand and debris, however, I realized that a part of my pile was moving. Upon closer inspection, I realized that it contained dozens of tiny, white maggots. I reeled back, suppressing the urge to scream, only to step into another wriggling mass of them. I jumped, looking down and realizing that the ground was crawling with them. I decided to make an attempt at sweeping them away. Taking careful steps through the small kitchen, I moved them in little groups toward the door. I looked back down, horrified to see all of my piles writhing and wriggling into one another.

Unable to continue, I flung open the door, stormed out, and screamed to the ocean. Seagulls screamed back. Waves crashed. The wind blew. I looked all around at the grey, cloudy sky, wishing with all that I was that I might be anywhere but there.

Resigned to my fate, I returned indoors to finish

my task, only to find that it had somehow finished itself for me. Not one trace of the maggots remained. I searched for some place they might have gone, but I was not able to find one.

Brantley continued to "work" late into the night, skipping dinner (as well as his promised flounder fishing) and ignoring all of my calls for him to come down from the tower. Knowing better than to go up there again, I went to bed without him, with Neptune at my feet. Sleep came surprisingly fast, and all thoughts of the day left me as my mind drifted into a distant region of its own design.

I was back in Norland, attending a masquerade ball. I wore a heavy dress, the many layers of pink and white silk making my gait slow yet elegant. I wore matching slippers and long white gloves, and I held before my face an elaborately adorned mask. I moved among the dancing guests, searching the masks, wondering where Brantley was. The room was a mass of spinning gowns and extravagant costumes of every imaginable color and fabric. The masks were all thoroughly concealing, so that no one could identify anyone else by sight alone.

I turned as someone behind me tapped my shoulder.

"May I have this dance?" the man asked in an unfamiliar voice as he bowed.

I replied with a nod and a curtsey, and the two of us began to move along with the rest of the guests. The song was a lovely waltz, and everyone danced accordingly.

"Do you know the lord of this estate?" my dancing partner asked me, his hand brushing my hip as we circled once.

"I don't believe so," I answered, realizing that I did not recognize the dance hall.

"I was not invited either," he said.

"I can't say if I was invited or not," I said, a strange feeling coming over me. It was as if I no longer felt like I belonged there. I felt alone and vulnerable, like I had come by mistake and my secret was soon to be revealed. "I must go," I said, then politely curtseyed and hurried off.

To my surprise, my dancing partner followed right behind me. He stopped me at the door. "Are you sure you don't want to stay for tonight's festivities?"

I nodded. "Quite sure."

He bowed humbly. "Until we meet again," he said, lowering his mask just enough to show me the face beneath. It wasn't a face at all, though, but the rotting skull of a corpse. Maggots writhed from his eye sockets, his nose was blackened and hallow, and his mouth hung from the ghastly mass by some supernatural means. As he came back up, so did his mask, and he turned from me and disappeared into the dance.

My heart racing, I flung open the door and rushed out. Suddenly, I was at sea, standing just outside the captain's quarters among a small crew on an unfamiliar vessel. We fought heavy winds and powerful waves.

"*Moskoe-ström!*" one of the men yelled.

I turned to see that we headed directly for a giant whirlpool. The ship sped as it fell into the vortex, and I watched as the crew worked frantically to direct it free. There was no use, though, and moments later, the *Maelström* swallowed us all.

I clung to the nearest bow as the ship plunged deep into the sea, and I watched as we spun ever deeper, the ship's crew floating off as one by one they drowned. I struggled to continue holding my breath, but then realized that it would be impossible for me to swim back up to the surface in time. I left a small trail of bubbles as the last of my air escaped my lungs. The urge to breathe forced water in its place, and I gagged and choked as the darkness descended upon me.

No sooner had I resigned myself to the fact that I was drowning, I felt arms on me, pulling me to the surface, then the painful shock of air as it hit my water-filled lungs. I began to cough uncontrollably, purging the liquid from my body, my nose running. I tried to sit up, but I found that I was too exhausted. I strained to focus my eyes, still burning from the salt, when I realized that Brantley knelt over me, dripping wet and gasping for breath, his head haloed by the rising sunlight breaking through the morning fog.

"Karina! What were you doing?"

I shook my head, equally confused as he was. I lay on my side, water still finding its way out of me. I shivered, realizing how cold I was. Waves crashed in the distance, but I could not see them through the fog. I found the strength to sit up and dust the excess sand from my hair.

"Karina?"

I turned to him, unable to mask my confusion.

"Are you all right?" he asked, catching his breath.

I shook my head. "What happened?"

He looked down, a strange combination of fear

and anger contorting his face. "I told you not to go walking alone in the fog! I shudder to think of what may have become of you had I not woke to use the outhouse!"

"But I wasn't out walking! I have no idea how I got out here!"

A look of realization hit him. "You were moving about in your sleep!"

"Somnambulating?" I looked around, watching the fog slowly thin as more and more hints of sunlight began to break through.

He lifted me into his arms and carried me back to the lighthouse. I grasped him tightly around the neck, unable to stop shivering. I lay in bed, trembling beneath the blankets, my wet dress crumpled on the floor.

"You're all right now," he said.

I gave him a sideways glance, unable to mask my confusion. Was either of us all right? I tried to look him in the eyes, finding that I still could not.

"I have some things I need to take care of," he said, and my heart sank as he disappeared up the staircase.

He remained up there for some time. When he finally emerged, he moved all about the lighthouse, up the stairs, through the lamp tower, back down the stairs, growling and mumbling to himself. I wanted to ask him what was wrong, but I dared not utter a word.

Chapter Five

"**K**arina!" his voice echoed down the tall spiral staircase, a deep and angry intonation sending a foreboding chill through me.

I wrapped my robe around me as I moved to the foot of the stairs and looked up. He stared down at me through the tower door, his eyes wild and his shirt soaked with sweat along the chest and underarms. His hair was a greasy mass, with short blond locks set about his head like spines or horns. There was something familiar about the sight, although I could not place it.

"What did you do with it?" he growled, prompting Neptune to jump to his feet with the fur on his back raised on-end.

"With what?" I asked, genuinely confused.

He wiped the sweat from his brow with an annoyed flick of his hand. "You know ex*act*ly what I'm talking about! Where is it?"

I shook my head, the look in his eyes as he

continued to stare me down causing my throat to go tight. "I have no idea what you're talking about!"

He took a few steps down, but he stopped as Neptune barked. His glance shifted to the dog, then slowly back to me. "Get him out of here. We need to talk—in peace."

"I would prefer to keep him here," I said.

He cocked his head, strangely surprised by my response. "You would *prefer* to keep him in here?"

I nodded.

He took a few more steps down. "*You* would pre*fer* it?"

I continued to nod, a stifling terror gripping me, arresting my breath. What madness had taken hold of him up there I cannot say, but I identified the danger that now stepped down toward me, and I realized I needed to get away. I rushed for the door, and Neptune went wild as Brantley raced down the steps.

I lunged open the door and ran out, pulling my robe tightly around me as I entered the late evening fog. A full moon filtered through, offering some light, although it helped little with the visibility. The little it illuminated it also cloaked in its rolling mist, so I ran with the same fearful abandon I had been forced to employ during my night in the forest. I stumbled over rocks and inconsistencies in the sand, but continued forward in search of the boat.

A light cry escaped me as I heard Neptune's barks suddenly muffled by a heavy slam of the lighthouse door.

"Karina!" Brantley yelled.

I scrambled forward, my lungs going heavy as I struggled to quiet my breaths. I wanted to cry aloud, the horror of this new event clouding and confounding my mind. I hit the beach, then began searching for the boat.

"Karina!" he yelled again, his voice sounding far closer than it should have.

I gasped as an unexpected rush of cold water hit my feet. I moved a few steps closer inland as I followed the edge of the tide. The fog shifted and I caught a glimpse of the boat just ahead, but for only a moment. I darted toward it.

"Stop!" Brantley yelled, as he reached for my hair.

His fingers brushed up against a lock, and then a moment later, the bruising sensation of a sudden, tearing tug sent me to my back. He immediately sat upon my chest, his weight making it difficult for my tired lungs to catch a breath.

"What are you trying to do to me?" he asked, staring down at me through bloodshot eyes, stinking of rum.

"I'm not trying anything!" I said with struggled breath.

His hands went to my throat. "Don't you want me to succeed?"

I tried to pry away his fingers, but his grip was too firm. "Please!" I managed to utter.

"Where did you put it? Tell me now!"

I shook my head, tearing at his hands with my fingernails, kicking my legs, all in vain. I tried to cry out another plea, but gagged and choked instead. I felt my eyelids flutter, my mouth agape in a last desperate appeal for air, and then I watched as everything went quiet and the darkness slowly consumed the fog.

Yet the darkness did not consume everything. Then, slowly, the fog began to reemerge until once again the fine, white mist surrounded me. Something prompted me to walk, and I realized that my bare feet brushed through not sand, but grass. I began to scrutinize my surroundings, making out the vague outlines of pine trees.

How had I gotten in the forest?

I shrieked with a start as an enormous moth flew before my face. I cringed back, my hands flying forward to knock it away, its size and the detail of its features from my close vantage bringing about a most terrible blow to my senses. The moth had wings of gold, the scales shiny and distinct, and as it flew, its wings sounded like those of a little bird. The most distinct characteristic of the moth, however, was the skull it brandished across its back, clear as anything else, as if my own personal omen.

Death.

A flash of recollection hit me, and I remembered Brantley pinning me to my back on the foggy beach, strangling me. Was I now dead? I wondered if I was now nothing more than a wandering spirit, damned to some kind of purgatory because of my unnatural end. I glanced down at my body, feeling my arms with their opposite hands. They felt solid. Weren't spirits merely apparitions, even in form? I pinched the flesh of my left wrist, noting the pain. I was clearly more than an apparition, but that did not at all help to explain how I got to the forest.

I had no choice but to move forward, unsure what direction I was even going. Although the fog carried a certain luminescence to it, there was no discernable moonlight. I could see a few steps ahead of me, and no further, but I could see well enough to walk at a brisk pace without stumbling or tripping over divots and emerging tree roots. Also, I noticed that the air was cool but comfortable. I was able to cover much ground in a satisfying span of time, and I walked confidently, as if my destination were clear.

I noticed a light up ahead and wondered if perhaps I might be so lucky as to run into my treasure-hunting friends. Without changing my pace, I veered toward the light. Soon, I was close enough to see the source, and I ducked behind a tree to get a closer look. The lamp that had beckoned me hung from the tip of a long branch. An enormous wooden table seated with twelve men and women stretched below it. The table had on it the largest feast I had ever seen. There were game birds large and small, a whole pig still on the rotisserie, bowls overflowing with fruits of all colors and shapes, boiled corn, potatoes, and carrots, numerous kinds of bread and cheese, and an array of sweet desserts. There were numerous bottles of open wine, both white and red, and no one had an empty glass.

I looked at the various guests seated at the table. There were more men than women, seven to five, and there appeared to be but one couple amongst them all. One empty seat stood near one end of the table. The men wore suits, tattered and ill sized as they were, and the women wore dresses, none in any better condition than mine. They presented the most unusual visual dichotomy: peasants enjoying more food than they could possibly eat. I wondered how this could be and considered the possibility that I had stumbled across a troupe of bandits. I ducked back behind the tree, planning my retreat, when one of the women came up behind me.

"Welcome!" she said.

I turned to her, my heart racing as I struggled to produce a friendly smile. "Hello."

"We were just sitting down for a late supper. Won't you join us? We have room for one more," she said, pointing to the open thirteenth seat.

I looked back at the seat, then at the others sitting around the table. The group stared back, every one of them silently awaiting my reply.

"We have plenty of food," said the woman.

I nodded, fearing the possible repercussions of refusing the offer, and everyone looked satisfied as I took the empty seat and surveyed the spread of food. I couldn't place it yet, but something was not quite right about it all. I caught a whiff of something foul and began to search for its source.

"Have some turkey," said another one of the women. She stood to serve me a piece. "And some boiled potatoes."

I watched as she added the items to my plate, holding my breath as I realized the meat was rancid and the potatoes moldy.

"And have some cheese and crackers," said another, coughing into her hand before grabbing a handful of each for me. The crackers crumbled in her grasp and the moldy cheese oozed between her fingers.

"And you must have some of our best wine," said one of the men. He jumped to his feet and grabbed the nearest bottle, then filled my glass with a white wine that had been sitting so long that it now gave off the unmistakable aroma of vinegar.

"Thank you. I don't know where to start," I said, looking over the inedible display.

"Tell us: what brought you to our patch of the forest?" the man with the vinegar asked. He topped off his own glass, and then sniffed its contents with decadent abandon. "Fine year!"

"Indeed!" said a man seated near him with a raise of his glass. The two toasted and took hefty swigs.

I found all eyes shifting to me as I struggled to remember how I had gotten to the forest. "I somnambulated here," I guessed aloud.

"Somnambulated?" a couple of them repeated with surprise and disbelief.

"I somnambulate sometimes," I added, hoping to satisfy their suspicions.

Few of them looked convinced. One of the few stood, however, with an intent look to his face. He was a tall, skinny man with dark hair and clothing meant for someone at least a foot or two shorter than he was. His face was slightly obscured by the beginnings of a beard and mustache, but still I could see that he had a kind smile. "I believe her," he said.

The group turned its attention to him.

"We all came here by chance, didn't we?" he asked.

A low mumble flooded over the table as everyone began whispering at once. I tried to make out what the various people were saying, but I could only discern what came from those closest to me: "He has a point"; "She has an honest face"; "Did you hear her accent?"; "I'll bet you all of the coins in my pocket that she's here to ruin us all."

I strained to continue looking calm, but I knew I had no choice but to sit there and wait for them to decide what they thought of me. Had I run, I would have appeared guilty of whatever the paranoid one thought I was up to, and there was no way I would have been able to outrun everyone there. I remained quiet as the group discussed me, two or three of the members talking as if I weren't even there. My alarm grew as I made out a few other pieces of discourse: "She looks nervous"; "Why won't she eat?"; "I wonder if she's a tease?"

Understanding that I had no other option, I stood to address the rest of the table. "Ladies and gentlemen," I began. I cleared my throat. "I have been through more tonight than any woman deserves to go through. I'm tired and in no mood for festivities, so if you would be so kind as to excuse me—"

"Madame," interjected the man with the vinegar. "How can you claim to have been through so much, yet also maintain that you cannot remember why you're here?"

I shrugged, searching for an answer.

"Who sent you?" the paranoid one asked, his eyes suddenly piercing and intent as he stared me down.

I pushed back my chair, fearing I might have no choice but to run, despite my odds of outracing any pursuers. "No one!"

"No one?" a small group of them repeated with heavy suspicion.

About half of the group rose from their seats, ready to follow me, but the paranoid man pulled out a loaded and readied pistol.

He pointed it at my forehead. "You are by far the rudest guest I've ever encountered."

"I'm sorry if I have offended you," I said, my eyes fixed on the end of the malevolent barrel.

"Dinner's ruined!" he said, and I winced in anticipation of the shot.

Instead of shooting me, he shifted his aim to the lantern. Glass suddenly shattered and there was an explosion of flames and screams across the table, but much to my surprise, everything then went cold and dark. I felt weightless as everything else seemed to fall out of existence. The fog drifted into the distance until I could no longer see anything but the blackness now depriving me of every sense.

Suddenly, my senses returned to me and realized that I lay in some kind of box. I smelled cedar, recognizing the smell and realizing that somehow I had become enclosed in my clothing trunk. I searched my throbbing head for some clue as to how I had gotten there. Brantley. . . . My elbow hit the side as I reached my hand to my throat. Yes, I remembered it now . . . Brantley had strangled me.

I hit the wooden lid in front of me, finding it weighted down. A small amount of sand fell from overhead. "Brantley!" I screamed.

No one responded. The muffled sound continued. I listened to it carefully, but I was unable to determine its source. I felt the wood against my back, analyzing the sensation of wet sand against my fingertips. I found that I could smell it too, and a fishy hint of brine. I screamed again as I felt something suddenly move beside my leg. I tried to sweep it away, grazing a cold and scaly tailfin before slapping my knuckles against the hard cedar.

A *fish?* After I had begged Brantley to catch a flounder for supper, he had finally caught one, but for what? To spite me? To stink up the box?

A thrilling terror tore through my body as I realized that Brantley had buried me alive. Moreover, given the amount of water seeping into the bottom of my makeshift coffin, I could only speculate how dangerously near I was to the water's edge. I knew from the brightness of the rising moonlight I observed earlier that the high tide was due, but because of my blackout, I had no way of knowing just how late it was.

I pounded my fists against the weighted door again and more sand sprinkled down with each strike. Sand dropped over my face, some catching my nose and mouth, some finding my eyes, and I shied back, my sandy fingers unable to assist me.

"Help!" I cried as loudly as I could. "Please help!"

I felt my air growing thin. My eye burned, and I held it closed, convincing myself the sand was the sole source to my tears. I shivered, the damp sand against my back permeating a chill deep into the core of my being. The thought finally hit me that I likely had no alternative but to lie there until I either suffocated or drowned, and I drew my arms around myself, desperate for the semblance of warmth and comfort.

The sound suddenly grew clearer, and I realized it was not one sound but two. One was the breaking of nearby waves, and the other was . . . digging?

"Brantley, is that you?" I cried.

No one responded. The digging sound paused for a few seconds and continued.

Although he obviously meant to kill me (if he had not mistaken me for dead before deciding to dispose of my body), I held out hope that I might somehow reach him before he had completed the deed. "Please let me out! I promise I'll return to Norland and you'll never hear from me again! I won't speak a word of this to anyone! Please, Brantley!"

The digging continued.

"Please, I'm begging you! I don't want to die!"

Still, the digging continued. I allowed myself to sob aloud, desperation hitting me as my hope shattered. I felt the cold tingle of water rising against my back, and I knew the high tide was well on its way. I had mere minutes before the water level would rise over me, just minutes before a cold and agonizing death, and I had no choice but to resign myself to it.

My mind shifted from me to my family, and I wondered if they would ever know the truth—to everything. Would word eventually come to them of my death, or would Brantley be able to feign some elusive phantom of my existence long after I had gone? Would Mother think America had made me forget her? Would they ever find the body Brantley had hidden down in the walls of our wine cellar?

I wondered if ultimately that was the cause of his madness. No doubt, murder changes a person. I wouldn't know firsthand, as I was a mere accessory after the fact, but that fateful night still burned through the back of my mind.

Brantley had been drinking with the help again

when the footman took him aside and gave his demands. He threatened to make up a scandal between Brantley and the footman's sister Greta, who came with him to their estate whenever the help needed an extra set of hands. That the two would conspire against him in such a way had been insulting enough, but the amount of money they felt they were due had been ridiculous—or so Brantley had said. I was not in the room at the time, so I cannot say how reliable the story actually was; however, after seeing how quickly Brantley turned on me, I'm less inclined to consider his innocence.

He had sent away the servants for the evening, telling them he intended to have a quiet night with his wife, giving the impression that he was sending the footman away with the rest. He took the man aside as the small group disseminated, however, secretly reeling him back inside with the promise of a suitable proposal. Of course, the two men drank another bottle of wine before Brantley took him downstairs, and by the time I got down there, the deed had already been done. The body was already half entombed in the wall. I merely helped Brantley finish the masonry. It had been an awful task, but he had convinced me that it was for the best. Together, we finished the new wall, back in a far, oddly-shaped corner no one would notice was suddenly a few bricks wider. Just the same, we both agreed we would not ask the servants to bring up any wine for a few days and, in the meanwhile, we would confuse their sense of space with an order to rearrange the furniture in all of the regularly used rooms.

The plan had worked well, but still people had

their questions about the footman's disappearance. Inspectors came to check the property, and of course, they found nothing. We held off on finding a replacement, hoping to give others the impression that we awaited his safe return. When there could be no more denying that the man was not coming back, Brantley feigned an investigation of his own and looked genuinely dumbfounded when no leads came. He made me stay silent during his ruses, as my acting capabilities—so he said—were hideous.

About a week after we buried the footman in our wine cellar wall, the reek of decay began to permeate through. Brantley had made certain that our masonry held as it should, but not even brick and mortar could hide the stench of death. Luckily, it was faint enough at first and the servants assumed it was a dead rat. They could have been right, but Brantley and I both knew better.

It was around that time when Brantley began talking about the lighthouse.

"It is an opportunity we will never see again!" he insisted.

"And what about our life here?" I asked.

"Our life here is crumbling!" was his response. "You know it's only a matter of time before we're found out. We best seal up the estate for a good ten or twenty years—"

"You want to spend the next twenty years in America?" I interrupted.

"We have no choice!"

My gut had told me even then that something was amiss in his reasoning, that no sane person would move his wife across the ocean to live in a *lighthouse*, but for whatever reason, I held faith in him. And where had that faith put me?

I listened to the crash of the waves, each seemingly louder and higher than the last. The water entered my coffin more quickly than it left, and I found myself pressing up against the lid for the little, thin air that remained. The digging had continued for as long as I could hear, but my ears now lay permanently underwater, bombarded by the nonstop thundering of the sea, so I could not be sure if Brantley remained. I said a prayer, water entering my mouth and reaching for my nostrils. In one last, desperate move for air, I pressed my face as hard as I could against the wooden surface above me. To my surprise, it gave.

I slammed both hands against it, and the hinged top lifted. I threw it open and sat up with a wild gasp, shocked to find Neptune at my side. I moved to embrace the dog, but he lunged for the dead flounder at my side and immediately ran off with the treasure he had so voraciously dug after.

I sat there for a few minutes, contemplating. I considered my chances if I returned to confront Brantley, although deep down I knew it would be best to find the boat and leave him to his cursed lighthouse. A peculiarity stopped me in my tracks, however, one that spoke of the trouble now most certainly waiting within: the lamp had gone out.

Chapter Six

I began my way back through the darkness just as it began to rain, which further obscured my view. I moved as quickly as I could, feeling my way to the base of the lighthouse, my hand trembling as I reached for the door. My hair began to dance through the misty air and the wind pressed my sleeves and skirt to my skin. There was a dangerously nearby flash of lightning and almost an immediate crash of thunder as I opened the door. I hurried inside, further shaken by what I knew had to be a near miss.

I took a moment to catch my breath, unnerved by the silence. I wondered if Brantley had abandoned this place as well, unwilling to be found within the vicinity of my body if it happened to dislodge and wash ashore. I moved to the foot of the staircase.

"Brantley?" I called.

No response.

I looked up as another thundering crash of lightning hit nearby, the sky illuminating just long enough for me to catch a glimpse of the hanging body. I staggered back, my hand going to my mouth, a gripping mesh of dread and relief seizing me. I looked back up, barely able to make out the image in the dark room. The thought crossed my mind that I could have imagined the body, that all I had endured that night could have twisted my mind and brought about a delusion.

"Brantley!" I yelled up the steps.

He did not reply, although that in itself was not unusual. Still, he never would have allowed the lamp to go out. For whatever reason he had brought us here, he had taken his job as lighthouse keeper seriously.

I took a deep breath and ascended the steps, my movements slow and cautious. Although I already knew that I had not been delusional, or even mistaken, a part of me did still expect Brantley to stop me as I approached the open tower door. Just the same, the body became more visible with each step, a small patch of moonlight entering the tower and offering some illumination.

I slowed even more as I neared it. He had attached one of our bed sheets to the top of the staircase, to the railing protecting the edge of a short platform that overlooked the rest of the spiral. I stopped as I stood directly over the body, leaning over the rail to look down at it. It swayed just slightly. Below it, the staircase seemed to spiral down into oblivion. A wave of dizziness took me, and I closed my eyes, grasping tightly to the railing.

As soon as I felt I could, I staggered back from the platform and turned to the tower door. It took me a moment to summon the will to cross the threshold, and my heart pounded wildly against my chest when I finally did. I struggled to breathe, my body wanting to collapse, as I stood in the circular room, staring out at the rainy night.

Lightning flashed again, and for that moment, I witnessed a glimpse of the madness that had driven my poor Brantley to his final days. Thunder rumbled as I reflected upon the images in my mind's eye. Along the wall, just below the windows that offered a 360-degree view of the ocean and coastline, there were words, pictures, and lines connecting them all with seemingly no rhyme or reason. Much of it seemed to have been a longstanding endeavor made with pen and ink, although to my horror, some of the words were written in blood. The letters ran down the wall, as if the wall itself were bleeding the words.

Lightning lit the room and, for another quick moment, I took in as much of the wall as I could. Among the words and phrases written in blood were: *spectacles*; *Wilson*; *The Ragged Mountains*; *the raven*; and *premature burial*. From "spectacles" was a line drawn to the ink-written names "Professor Feather" and "Dr. Tarr." Drawn from "Wilson" was a line connecting it to "devil in the belfry." "The Ragged Mountains" and "the raven" had a line connecting the two to one another, and then lines connecting them to nearly every other word or phrase near them. Thunder rumbled in the distance, sending a sudden shudder through me. I staggered back a few steps and hit Brantley's flimsy desk with my thigh, nearly falling over with the impact. Lightning struck again.

That's when I noticed the letter.

It was sealed with a dab of unmarked wax and addressed to a Mr. Poe in Baltimore. I tried to peek without compromising the wax as the next lightning strike came, but without success. I considered breaking the seal, rationalizing that I might reseal it once I'd had a chance to look at the contents. Finally, I decided that whatever Brantley had written, it had been for Mr. Poe's eyes, not mine. Despite all Brantley had put me through—or perhaps because of it—I decided I would deliver the letter, face this man, whoever he was, and find out what he knew about the lighthouse.

I bundled as many changes of clothes as I could carry over one shoulder, then gathered as many food items as I could haul over the other in my apron. I returned to the office and rummaged through the desk, finding a small bag of money. With some trepidation, I returned to Brantley's hanging body. I held my breath as I turned him to face me. I forced myself to breathe.

"This is goodbye, my love," I whispered.

My hands shaking, I took his pocket watch. With another thought, I twisted the wedding ring off his cold, stiff finger and dropped both into my skirt pocket. I did not want the mementos, but I did need the travel funds.

After only a short amount of consideration, I left him hanging, deciding he deserved to rot there.

I called for Neptune, and he appeared from seemingly nowhere, content and ready to follow me to the boat.

I questioned my decision to leave immediately as soon as we hit the open water, but by then it was already too late. The waves were shallow, but violent, throwing the little boat far from any shore. Lightning flashed overhead, and for a moment, I was positive I would be hit, but I realized the activity was confined to the thick cloud cover, as frighteningly close as it appeared to be. I began to row, but it seemed that I wanted to go in the exact opposite direction as nature wanted to take me and I had no choice but to concede. By luck, the boat stayed afloat and both Neptune and I found our way to solid land.

It was impossible to say at first where we had hit the shore, but we simultaneously fled the boat as soon as we could see the sandy ground. I waded through the last stretches of the high tide's waves, caring no longer about ruining the silk of my tattered dress or losing the ribbons in my hair. My freedom from that terrible lighthouse was my only thought, each step I took away from it feeling even more liberating than the last.

I collapsed as I hit the dry sand, suddenly realizing how much the past several hours had taken out of me. The cold air against my wet skin was excruciating, but I stayed where I was, shivering, huddled in the sand. Neptune had to have sensed my distress, as he circled me for a couple of minutes, then lay down beside me. The warmth of his body eased the biting cold, and I felt myself begin to relax a bit.

A tired daze took over me. I had no idea what time it was, but it was certainly late. My muscles burned as I moved to get up and escape the cold, drenching rain, and I collapsed almost immediately. I could go no further. I had pushed my body to its limit, and all I could do was lie there and wait for my strength to return. I lay in silent contemplation for some time.

My mind kept wandering back to Brantley and the lighthouse, no matter where else I tried to send it. What had those words on the walls meant? What did he think they had to do with the local legend of the buried treasure? Perhaps he had simply been insane the entire time, hiding the worst of it for last. That was possible.

I wondered how much of it even mattered now. He had taken his life after believing he had taken mine, and before that, he had taken the life of our footman. And he had claimed to come from noble blood! I laughed aloud at the thought. How he had fooled me! How he had fooled everyone.

It occurred to me that I was crying, and I turned to the sky, allowing the rain to wash away my tears. Neptune got to his feet, sniffing the air. He leaned against me and licked my face, prompting me to my feet. My muscles were tight and weary, but my exhaustion had passed. I wiped my face with my shirtsleeve and shook as much sand as I could from my skirt. Despite the continuing rain, there were breaks in the clouds where patches of moonlight broke through and allowed some visibility. With little hesitation, I grabbed my belongings and began toward town.

Neptune stayed close, running ahead every once in a while, then falling back to my side as he sniffed and examined our path. There was an excitement about him, his tail flopping wildly in his wake, hitting my skirt whenever he passed me. I supposed he might have been in a good mood because of the fish dinner he'd recently eaten, but it seemed more to me that he was genuinely eager to get to where we were headed.

I walked as quickly as my tired limbs would permit, which I could tell frustrated the hound a bit. He sprinted ahead a few times, only to circle back and hurry off again. He eventually ended up back beside me, but it was evident that his patience was wearing thin.

"I know," I told him with a pat to the head. "I want to get out of this rain just as badly as you do."

My voice reassured him for a short while. Then, to my surprise, he darted ahead and did not return. As I searched for him, I noticed the town's lights not too far off. I tried to hurry my pace, but my exhaustion far exceeded my excitement. My back was tired and tight, my legs had grown impossibly heavy, and I began to wonder if I had it in me to reach town, as close as I now was to it. My determination drove me forward. I dragged my feet, laboring to complete each step, holding my eyes on the goal up ahead. I watched it get closer, step by agonizing step. As I neared the town's edge, I heard Neptune's familiar gait. He trotted eagerly toward me.

"I was afraid you had left me for good," I said as he let me pet him.

He turned around and led the way, running back and forth again as if it might somehow make me walk faster.

"We'll get there when we get there," I said as if he might somehow understand.

He continued running his impatient circles until we were surrounded by buildings. The inn was nearby, and not too far from that was the market street. Neptune eagerly led the way.

Only a few patrons drank at the bar, and one man ate some kind of meat with fried potatoes. Neptune ran to the fire still raging in the fireplace as I looked for the innkeeper, praying he would not turn me away. The man, also the barkeep, emerged from a back room, a look of recognition coming to him as he saw me and my dog.

"I didn't expect to see you here again, especially at this hour," he said, pouring me a drink.

Surprised but gracious, I accepted the drink and swallowed it down with a wince.

"You left so early last time I never had the chance to thank you. While you were sleeping, that hound of yours chased off what turned out to be an outlaw. That's one exceptional dog you have there. Saved my life, I'm sure," said the innkeeper.

I glanced over at Neptune, who now lay quietly in the warm glow of the fire, then back at the innkeeper. "He's definitely special, like someone sent me a guardian angel. Would you believe he's saved my life as well—twice, in fact?"

The innkeeper nodded. "You trained him well."

I smiled, deciding it best to keep my brief history with the dog to myself.

"He's free to sleep by my fireplace anytime, and for no charge of course," the man said, pouring me another drink.

I nodded my thanks.

"Tonight, you're both my honored guests. Whatever you need, just let me know."

I drank the second shot and set the glass aside. "Do you think you could arrange a hot bath?"

To my fortune, the inn had a bathtub on the premises, the water already heated. The small tub room was cold, the tile floor wet and slick, a shudder rushing up my body as I stepped into the steaming bath. The contrast of the heat against the cold was delightful, but as my body warmed and I began to wash away the sand and brine, I felt myself finally beginning to relax. I closed my eyes and drew my head underwater to rinse my hair. When I surfaced, I found my lamp had gone out. I turned as I thought I saw something moving, but it proved merely to be a shadow playing with the edges of my vision.

I felt curiously unnerved and couldn't bear the thought of being alone. I tried to assure myself that my panic was unfounded, that I was safe here, but I could not shake the uneasy feeling that my safety no longer existed anywhere. I dried and dressed as quickly as I could, then I returned to the inn's dining room. Instead of going upstairs to my room, I crossed to the fireplace. Neptune raised his head to look at me with a wag of his tail, happy to share the dwindling firelight. I rested as close as I could to him and, feeling secure for the first time in months, I slept a sound and dreamless sleep.

Chapter Seven

I woke the next morning with the sun, the heralding of a rooster echoing from somewhere nearby. I dressed quickly, determined to get an early start to the railway station, only to find that the innkeeper's wife had prepared breakfast. I could not refuse the generous offering, which included rye bread fresh from the oven, fried potatoes, fresh eggs, and cuts of cheese. The couple also happily fed Neptune, and even offered to keep him for me while I sought out sales and supplies throughout the town's handful of venues.

My first order of business was to see about selling Brantley's pocket watch and wedding band. The general store was only a short walk away, and was clearly marked by a sign above its veranda's eaves. The building consisted of two stories, both whitewashed with brown trim. As I stepped up to the wooden veranda, a short, sleight man wearing an apron over his suit greeted me with a smile. He was older, with graying hair and a short beard, but he had striking blue eyes that seemed to illuminate as he addressed me.

"Good morning, Madame!"

I gave him a nod. "Good morning, sir."

He watched me as I looked around the small store. There were shelves of grain, corn, and other food staples, as well as medical supplies, tobacco, and alcohol. Various odds and ends filled the rest of the place, with tools, yarn, brushes, and even some barnyard supplies taking up random bits of shelf space. The storekeeper followed me as I moved to the counter beside the cash register.

"What can I do for you?" he asked.

The question bringing upon me a newfound sense of hesitation, I dug into the pocket of my skirt and felt the watch and ring within it for a moment. I felt the contours around the watch, its flimsy connection to the matching gold chain, and the ten perfectly even links between it and its fastener. The metal was cold and smooth, and I could feel the tick of the second hand through my fingertips. Then, getting louder with each click of the second, I could hear it. I grasped the ring, held it tightly, then released it back into the depths of my pocket.

"Are you all right?" asked the man behind the counter.

I looked up at him, summoning the strength to produce the watch from my pocket. I set it on the counter, watching it as I slid it away from me. "I was hoping I might sell this."

He took the watch into his hands and examined it closely. He did not seem to notice that its second hand continued to grow even louder.

Tick, tick, tick, tick. . . .

I felt my body go flush and sweaty, as if I were in the process of committing some terrible crime. I reminded myself that I was doing nothing wrong. Brantley had put me in this position. I had no choice but to sell the watch.

Tick, tick, tick, tick. . . .

"I'll give you five for it."

"Five? It's worth more than ten," I told him.

He shrugged. "I can give you five."

Tick, tick, tick, tick. . . .

I watched the clock, the minute hand moving from one second to the next, watching a minute pass, then another, each click of the hand like a drum in my ear.

"Six, then, and I'm not going any higher," he said.

I looked up at him, suddenly remembering to breathe. The seconds ticking by didn't seem to faze him, and I took a deep breath as I worked to collect my thoughts. Suddenly, the image of Brantley's body swinging in the tower flooded my mind, his eyes wide and his tongue protruding. His lifeless body hung awkwardly from his makeshift noose, and even in death, he seemed to be telling me something.

Tick, tick, tick, tick. . . .

"I'll give you six dollars and two bits, and no more," said the storekeeper.

I looked up at him, my heart racing as if in competition with the loud ticking of the watch. I took another deep breath, then gave the man a satisfied nod. "That will be fine." I felt through my pocket, finding the ring again. An unexpected jolt hit me as the storekeeper opened his register, however, and I dropped the ring once more.

The man handed over the small bounty, then collected the watch and chain. "Is there anything else I can do for you?"

I looked around, anxious to leave. I shook my head. "Thank you," I said before turning around and hurrying out of the building.

It was a relief to put some space between me and the watch, the sound of its second hand waning with every step I took away from it. As I exited the store, I felt as though I had freed myself from some enormous invisible net, the weight of it now discarded in my wake. I considered retuning to see if the storekeeper might also buy the ring, but my feet continued to carry me away from the building and back toward the inn.

Neptune greeted me as I entered, at ease with the innkeeper.

"Did you find what you needed?" asked the innkeeper.

I nodded. "Now I just need to find my way to the railway station. I have a long journey ahead."

"The railway station, you say? I've heard rail travel is terribly unsafe. Wouldn't you prefer a carriage?"

"I've travelled by rail before. It is much faster and far more comfortable."

He sighed. "Very well. I have a friend with a buggy who might be able to drive you," he said.

"I would appreciate that."

"Though, I doubt you'll be able to bring the hound with you into the railcar," he said.

I looked down, reflecting on the innkeeper's words. I hadn't considered the possibility that I might not be able to take Neptune with me. The thought of it stung a bit, and I took a few seconds to process my options.

"I would be happy to keep him here until your return," the man offered.

"I'm afraid I won't be coming back this way," I said, my throat going tight.

"Let me and the wife keep him then. I would hate for you to have to leave him behind as a stray."

I glanced back over at Neptune, who lay content by the fire. The innkeeper and his wife would treat him well, I knew, but at the same time, it pained me to think about parting with him. He was so loyal, so protective, and I did not want him to think I had left him despite his obedient and vigilant service.

I walked over to him and knelt at his side. "You're a good dog," I said, petting his head.

He wagged his clumsy tail, happy for the attention.

I stayed at his side for a few minutes, sad to let him go. By all rights, he was not even my dog. Who was I to remove him from this place?

"I'll miss you, boy," I told him, then stood and gathered my belongings. I turned to the innkeeper. "Thank you for everything."

"Thank *you*, my dear," he replied, walking me out. My heart sank as Neptune followed, and then sat protectively at my side while the innkeeper went to find his friend with the buggy.

Within a few minutes, he returned. At the innkeeper's side, high up on the buggy's seat, sat a good-looking young man. He held thick, leather reins, which extended to the bridle of an enormous, white stallion. The intimidating animal took a step to the side as I neared, strangely shaken by my presence. When I approached the driver, however, he gave me a welcoming smile.

"You must be Karina," he said.

I nodded. "And you are?"

"Ben."

The innkeeper walked up behind me. "I really appreciate this, Ben."

"My pleasure." He glanced back at me. "Ready to go?"

I nodded, albeit with some reluctance. The innkeeper walked me to the passenger door and opened it. I paused, turning to Neptune, then boarded the buggy. To my surprise, Neptune jumped up after me, immediately wriggling his way between Ben and me.

"Come on, now, Neptune," said the innkeeper. "You can't go."

Neptune refused to move.

"Come on out," the innkeeper tried again. He reached across me for Neptune's scruff, only to shy away when the dog replied with a forceful growl.

I turned to Neptune, just as surprised, although it was impressive how protective he was of me. I realized that, although I may not have claimed him as mine, he had claimed me the moment he had turned on his cruel master.

I turned back to the innkeeper. "I changed my mind. I want to bring him with me."

"And what if he cannot board the train?"

"Then we'll find some other way to Baltimore," I said.

His face went red and his eyebrows drew tightly

together. "That's ridiculous!" He looked over me, to Ben. "You don't want to travel with that hound at your side, I'm sure."

Ben shrugged. "I don't want to waste any more time sitting here while you two argue over it. Are we leaving?"

I nodded. The innkeeper reluctantly shut my door and stepped back as the buggy began down the road.

"I didn't mean to upset anyone," I said.

"He can get his own dog," Ben said.

I sat back, oddly reassured by the comment.

"So, Neptune is his name?"

I nodded. "Yes."

"Did you name him?"

"No. He belonged to another couple before me."

His face had a sense of bewilderment across it, and he seemed to contemplate something serious and weighty as he concentrated on the bumpy road. "Hmm."

I waited for him to add some kind of comment, but he said nothing.

The serious, thoughtful look remained fixed on him, prompting me to ask simply, "What?"

"What *what*?" he asked.

"That 'hmm' you made a moment ago."

He nodded. "I was just thinking."

"Yes?" I asked, growing impatient.

"I met a man years ago who had a dog named Neptune. His was a Weimaraner, though. Odd coincidence I'd encounter two dogs named Neptune out here."

"Odd indeed," I said, unimpressed.

"Sad story, his . . . at least so I heard. He went to

go live on that lighthouse at the coast just outside town."

"The Burnswatch lighthouse?" I asked, suddenly feeling uneasy.

"So you've heard the story?"

I shook my head. "No, but I . . . I've been by the lighthouse."

"Hmm," he said again.

Again, I waited to see if he might add something more meaningful, but he did not.

"What is the story?" I finally asked.

He quietly stared ahead for a short while, and then gave a thoughtful sigh. "I really don't think you want to hear it."

"Why is that?"

"It's quite gruesome."

I scoffed. "Gruesome!"

"You don't believe me?"

"I don't believe you want to share the story," I said plainly.

His lips went tight for a moment, but he finally conceded and told me the local tale of the Burnswatch lighthouse.

According to Ben, the lighthouse had been unoccupied for several months before Brantley's predecessor had finally taken the job. The lamp had been tended by a local fisherman during its vacancy, but the man had allowed the light to go out and tragedy had ensued. The rocky shallows had claimed dozens of lives, the ocean had collected their precious cargo of tea and spices, and all those involved in the periphery made it a priority to man the lighthouse with a proper keeper. The man they found had seemed the perfect fit. He was a widower, quite content with solitude, and he showed great enthusiasm over gaining the position at that particular lighthouse. Although he did not reveal any details, he had received a tip that the location held clues to the whereabouts of a treasure buried by shipwrecked pirates. Of course, legends of the kind were common all over in coastal regions and, among those who had lived in the area for any length of time, only the greatest of fools went around digging for buried treasure.

The man, whose name escaped Ben at the time he relayed the tale, had a dog named Neptune. The dog roamed the island freely, catching fish and guarding his owner. The man went to town once a week for supplies, always midday, and all seemed well at the lighthouse for a couple of months.

He began coming to town less often and buying increasing quantities of alcohol. Some of the local vendors began talking about the change they noticed in his character, noting that he had lost a considerable amount of weight. He had stopped smiling at some point, a permanent look of disgust etched across his lips, and he had gained an air about him that hinted at anticipation of something grave and frightful.

One of the last times anyone saw him alive, he had brought his dog with him. Both were gaunt, with tired looks in their sunken eyes. The dog carried a partially eaten piece of raw, bloody meat still on the bone. As the man moved through the market, a young vendor noticed upon closer inspection that the bloody mass was undoubtedly from a human thigh. The vendor tried to stop the man, only to provoke the dog and bring on an attack. The dog latched on to his leg, prompting other vendors to fend it off. The man and his dog fled together, and a small group of angry townspeople pursued, only to drop off, one by one, as the two retreated.

The vendor who had been bitten suffered a terrible infection in his leg, one from which he never recovered. He too began to waste away, an unexplained madness slowly taking hold of him. The more superstitious of townspeople began talking about a curse, something evil about the lighthouse that had begun to consume its keeper early into his employment. They believed whatever consumed him had begun also to consume the vendor who had tried to confront him, and a small group formed to go to the lighthouse and find a way to break the spell.

On a Sunday afternoon after church, the group carted another rowboat to the beach and four men crossed the short stretch to the island. They returned very shortly thereafter, all four pale and sick over what they had seen. They had confronted the man, only to find him raving mad, grunting like an animal and chasing the group with a knife. As they ran for the boat, they came across the dog's carcass, mutilated and partially dismembered, swarming with seagulls and maggots. Its jaw had been broken completely off and torn away from the rest of the head.

The group couldn't help but slow over the spectacle, which allowed the man to close the gap between them. They fought him away with their oars as they boarded the tiny boat, and he chased them into the cold water as they frantically rowed off. He stopped pursuing as the water reached his hips, stared at the group for a moment, then drove the knife deep into his own neck. The men watched as a spray of blood emerged from the wound, every beat of his heart pumping out more life from his shivering body. He lurched forward, a haunting smile replacing the longstanding look of disgust, spraying blood over the boat before collapsing into the water. The men watched, frozen by the display, as a pool of blood bubbled up, only to be washed away by the tide only a moment later.

To everyone's horror, a wave of madness tore through the town. People killed one another, mutilated themselves, starved and dehydrated to death, and committed suicide. A handful of people were committed to an asylum in a larger, adjoining town. None among those seemingly cursed with the lighthouse's plight lived long, and every one of them died a horrific death. Most people suspected some kind of plague, but some maintained that a true curse was to blame.

When Ben had finished relaying the story, all I could manage to utter in response was, "Hmm."

My sudden contemplation did not escape him, and with some surprise, he asked, "Hmm?"

"The man I got Neptune from, he had said something about the lighthouse being cursed. He must have named his dog after the one in the story," I said.

Ben shook his head. "It's a strange world, isn't it?"

"It truly is."

A look of reflection came over his face again and

he asked, "So, what sends you to Baltimore without your husband?"

I glanced down at the wedding band I still wore on my finger while my right hand went unconsciously into my pocket for Brantley's. I became aware of it as the metal hit my fingers, and a jolt of pain and anger stung me once more. "It's a personal matter," I finally said.

He nodded. "Forgive my intrusion."

Chapter Eight

I bought a train ticket to Baltimore and a box for Neptune in the cargo room. I claimed my seat then spent some time reflecting upon my decision to seek out this man, whoever he was. My husband had left behind a sealed envelope with his name on it, with instructions that it be hand-delivered. Although we had been on bad terms when he had passed, I still felt obligated to him.

I watched as the train moved through unknown territory. It was getting dark, so perhaps that was why the surrounding flats of farmland looked so ominous. A light rain caused my view of the outside to become distorted, the falling streaks separating the terrain in strange, jagged breaks, but still I stared out, watching, as I continued toward my destination.

I only closed my eyes for a moment, but when I opened them, there was a different passenger seated on my left. He was an older man with a short grey beard, and he watched me as though I were someone of interest. I looked around, noting that the densely seated car, which had been filled with passengers before I dozed, was now nearly empty. The lamps lighting the cabin had all burned away most of their fuel and now flickered angrily, sending their shadows dancing madly against every wall.

The older man beside me leaned in uncomfortably close. "Did I disturb your nap?"

"Do I know you?" I asked him.

He shrugged. "We could know each other."

I shook my head. "I don't think so."

"No?" He looked puzzled.

I sat back in my seat, hoping he might do the same.

He left me alone for a short while, but then he broke our silence with the strangest of questions: "If you were a cave, what kind of cave would you be?" The shadows behind him shuddered with new life.

"I beg your pardon?" I asked in reply, although I recognized the analogy immediately.

"I'm only asking a hypothetical question," he said, although the state of his pants said otherwise.

I turned away from him with a disgusted huff.

"I think yours would be a delicate, pretty cave," he said over my shoulder. "Long protected. Explored by few."

I pretended not to hear him, feigning the desire to take a nap in hopes that he might move on to another hapless target.

"If you want to go back to sleep, I can sit here and watch over you," he said.

"That won't be necessary, thank you."

"But what if the Bogey-Man comes through?" he asked as the lamp nearest to me burned completely out.

"The Bogey-Man?" I asked, holding my back to the man.

"He does terrible things to pretty young women like you. He just appears from the shadows, a specter in the night, leaving behind bloody carcasses in his wake."

"Why have I never heard of this Bogey-Man?"

"Perhaps it's because you're not from around here," he said.

It was obvious to anyone I spoke to that I was not from the area, and I knew very well that I was not in any more danger from some Bogey-Man than I was from the raving old man looming over me from the next seat.

To my surprise, he moved even closer. "Do you think I could tell you a story?"

"I would prefer to be left alone," I replied, trying my best to give a stern tone of voice.

"There was a man, whom I'll call Sam for the purposes of this story. Sam was a good family man, treated his wife well, and even had a baby on the way. But do you know what happened? Do you know, Madame . . . I'm sorry, but I didn't catch your name," he said.

"I didn't tell you my name, and I said I wasn't interested in your story."

"Well, I'll tell you what happened. The Bogey-Man got them," he said, speaking as if I had urged him on.

I rolled my eyes. "So terrible for them."

"He took a butcher knife to the wife, cut her up good, then—if you could believe it—he hanged the husband from the top landing overseeing their staircase."

I cringed, suddenly feeling sick and weak by the old man's presence. It was evident at this point that I was not dealing with a typical man, that he was quite possibly a deranged killer grooming his next victim. Another lamp violently flickered out. I wondered how the man would react if I excused myself to find an attendant, but then froze as he continued to speak.

"They both tried to outrun him, but that only made him angry, and when he was angry he became terribly cruel."

I swallowed hard, my throat going dry.

"The awful places a man can cut up a woman . . . just pure evil, this Bogey-Man. And do you think he would drop the man quickly and be done with him so fast? Do you?" he asked, placing a bony hand on my shoulder.

I shrugged away his hand and turned to face him, desperate to end his gruesome narrative. "I don't care! Please, go with your story and find someone else to tell it to!"

His eyes searched my face with surprise and contempt, and his lips went tight as he sat back. "My lady, you are precisely the type who should be listening to it—listening very, very carefully to it. Shall I tell you why?"

I stared him down, refusing him the satisfaction of a response.

"You should be listening because not all stories get to be heard by the *right people*," he said, looking around at the many empty seats throughout the cabin. "Do you understand what that means?"

I struggled to hold my stare, his proving far more commanding than mine. He had piercing blue eyes, and the deep wrinkles etched all along his face spoke of sights far more chilling than any sane man should ever be made to witness. The expression he held conveyed the horrible plans he had in mind for me. His exemplar story had planted the seeds of warning that he would not hesitate to kill the few others sitting among the empty seats, should I give him reason.

"What do you want from me?" I finally asked, unsure what else to say or do.

"I want you to *list*en to my story," he said, clenching his teeth.

Shadow filled the bulk of the cabin as yet another lamp's light went out.

I nodded, my eyes still firmly on his. "Fine, I'll listen. Tell me your story."

He sat back, looking satisfied for the moment. "I think the Bogey-Man is here, on this very train. Would you care to guess why?"

I shook my head.

"I deduced it," said the old man.

"I wouldn't know what that means," I said.

He cleared his throat. "Of course not. So then, I noted that the Bogey-Man had cut that poor woman to pieces and—wouldn't you know—I found this near the front of the train." He produced a butcher knife from the interior of his jacket. The knife had dried blood all along its sharp edge.

"Shouldn't you hand that over to a constable?" I asked, the sight of the knife making it difficult for me to breathe.

He shook his head. "I need more evidence first.

Perhaps if I were to come across another murder scene, that might be sufficient. Perhaps if the next one were more gruesome than the last, with more bodies and even more terrible things done to them, then I could take my evidence to the constable. Until then. . . ."

I flinched as his armed hand reached toward me, gasping as he placed his hand and the cold knife handle on my shoulder, holding the blade uncomfortably close to my neck. "Have you ever heard of one man burying another man behind a stone wall—while he was still alive?"

I shook my head, struggling to remain calm. The last lit lamp in the cabin flickered dimly, threatening complete darkness.

"That's what happened to the Bogey-Man, you know," he said. "A couple did it to him. They were a sly two. Do you know how they got him down into the basement?"

I shook my head.

"The husband got him drunk then offered the man a good time with his wife. Can you imagine that? A man using his wife as bait like that—and his wife being a willing participant? Can you imagine?"

I could feel the blood leave my cheeks, my breath going still, and yet I continued to shake my head.

"Who would have thought the man could have gone down so easily, just the blow of a wine bottle to the back of the head as she pretended to undress for him? With all that blood and red wine on the floor, who could have known he was still alive when the two began constructing his grave?"

"Where did you hear this story?" I asked, nearly

breathless.

"Why? Don't you like it?" he asked back.

"It's quite scary."

"Isn't it?"

"Especially with that knife right there," I said, cringing at my own brazen words.

He cocked his head, his face going flat, and the sharp blade suddenly fell flush against my throat. I thought to scream, but his eyes told me that any move would surely be my last. "What do you know about the Burnswatch lighthouse?"

With the cold metal pressing firmly against my skin, I found myself locked in indecision, afraid whatever answer I gave might provoke him further.

"I recently heard a legend," I told him.

"I don't care about legends. I care about facts," he said, pressing the blade terrifyingly hard as he adjusted its angle against my throat.

"I lived there for five months!" I cried. "I lived there with my husband Brantley. He went crazy there . . . but he's dead now. It's true what they say about the lighthouse. It *is* cursed."

"Was that so hard?" he asked, easing up slightly. When I did not reply, the knife went taut once more. "Was it?"

"No!"

"Good. Now, I do believe we were talking about the Bogey-Man before we got sidetracked with all of this other business. You might be interested to know that there is a connection between it all, nonetheless. What kind of connection, do you ask? Do you?"

I nodded.

"You see, the Bogey-Man went mad after only a

couple of days of being trapped between those walls. He had tried to break the crude masonry with his fists, only to bloody himself. Still, he continued to punch and lunge against the wall, determined to regain his freedom. Could you imagine the horror he must have felt after a day or so of being trapped in there? No light, no food or water, the threat of suffocation looming. . . . Could you imagine?"

I shook my head.

"Well, when he got out, his madness landed him immediately into an asylum, where his raving fits prompted the staff to do terrible, violent things to him. One can only imagine how those men only further fueled his madness. When he escaped, he swore his revenge, and sweet revenge he's had. Of course, he's not yet finished. He still has many people left to torture to death. Isn't that scary?"

I tried to say something, but found I was too terrified to speak. I swallowed hard, nearly choking.

"So where do you fit into all of this, you *might* ask," he said.

I shrugged, a light cry escaping me.

"Why don't you tell me?" He readied the knife against my throat, and I could tell that this time he meant to do real damage. I tried to back away from the blade's sudden bite, but he was too quick, and he sliced open my throat with a single hot stroke. I felt the warm blood flood down my body, then strangely go cold only moments after leaving my body. I felt everything grow colder as my arms and legs went numb. Everything went dark, then altogether black. I could hear the motion of the train for a few minutes, but then the rest of my senses also began to fade.

When my body had gone completely numb and my sense of hearing allowed only a muted echo of the sound around me, I heard him whisper into my ear, "You know I'm not finished with you yet, don't you?"

I sat up in my seat with a sudden gasp, my hands going to my throat. It took me a moment to realize that everything was intact. My throat had not been touched. There was not a trace of blood anywhere. The cabin was filled with other passengers.

The passenger to my left, an older woman with a kind face, asked, "Are you all right, my dear?"

I nodded. "Just a nightmare."

She sat back, satisfied, minding her business once more. I looked over her, hoping to distract myself with whatever I might see through the window. It was getting dark out, so I couldn't see much, but I could still make out the nearest trees and bushes as the train car passed them by.

I flinched back as something dark darted past the window. "Did you see that?" I asked the woman beside me.

She shook her head. "Did I see what?"

"I saw something fly past the window," I said.

"It was probably just a bird," she said.

Determined to repay the woman's previous neighborly conduct, I sat back and left it at that. When I saw the apparition pass by again, however, I sat forward and pointed. "There it was again! Did you see it that time?"

The woman gave an agitated huff. "I don't know what you're seeing, but I must ask you to kindly keep your observations to yourself."

"I'm terribly sorry to have bothered you, Madam," I said, sinking back into my chair.

She did not dignify me with a response, but instead turned back to her window and watched the fading view.

I dared not look again, so I turned to my right. A young man slept soundly in the seat on my other side. He had his head positioned at a painfully crooked angle, the shape of the cabin seats making sleep awkward at best. I decided to stare straight ahead for a while when the woman to my left began to scream.

I turned back to the window, and it took a moment for me to process the strange sight. An enormous black bird kicked and flapped its wings against the glass, somehow keeping in perfect time with the moving train.

"I think it's trying to get in, but it can't . . . can it?" the woman asked, shying back in her seat.

I watched, silent. The bird's wild, angry moves were hypnotic. I thought about my nightmare, about the impending doom promised to me, and I wondered if perhaps Death himself had been commissioned to track me down. No earthly bird would behave such a way, and I knew, given all I had recently seen, that was a personal omen if nothing else.

The woman frantically waved at the window, yelling for the bird to go away, but I watched silently, feeling quite assured that the bird was merely the harbinger of doom and not the actual purveyor of it. The woman's shrieks—not to mention the reactions of other nearby passengers—began to come across as comical overreactions to a threat that existed in their thoughts alone. The bird continued to harass the window, but clearly it had no way in. I sat back and watched the different reactions, wondering how many people the bird would alarm before it finally ducked away to carry its grim message to the next sorry soul on its list.

"Someone needs to scare it away," the old woman beside me finally suggested.

"It's attracted to something inside here," said someone else nearby.

"Or someone," said the old woman.

"What would a crow want with any of us?" I asked, my voice trembling despite me.

"That there is a raven," said the old woman.

"Whatever it is, what would it want with any of us?" I asked.

"Or we would ask, more specifically, what would it want with *you?*" the old woman asked. I realized that everyone in the car was staring at me. The raven continued to bat wildly against the glass. I tried to remain calm, but everyone began to move in toward me, giving me little room to shift. I felt a burst of nervous energy as the other passengers crowded all around me and suddenly I had no room to move at all.

Desperate for fresh air, the hot crowd leaving everything around me warm and stale, I attempted to push my way through. I could not see the door leading out, but I knew it was near. Each person I passed seemed to do his or her best to slow me down, grabbing at my clothes and blocking me with their bodies. After much grappling and groping, I finally made it to the door, only to find it locked.

The ride became unsteady, as if the train were suddenly traveling over heaps of rocks, then everyone screamed as we began to tilt to the left. I grabbed the nearest seat, doing my best to brace for the worst, when water broke through one of the windows. I watched a group of passengers fight the locked door while others attempted to flee through broken windows.

"*Maelström!*" one person cried.

Out here? I tried to make sense of it, realizing that it made no sense at all. I thought about a story I had read some time ago about a man who had thought he had awakened from a nightmare, only to realize that he was still dreaming. There was no other explanation in my mind that fit what I now witnessed, and I closed my eyes and allowed the water to rise over me, knowing very well that the dream would not be able to last much longer. I held my breath and shut my eyes as the current snatched my body and flung it into the sea. I felt my body float deep into the abyss below, bubbles rushing past me as they escaped the folds of my dress, my long curls tangling across my face.

The pressure against my lungs became great and the urge to exhale overcame me, but I couldn't even see the surface from where I was and I had nowhere to take a breath. Unable to hold the air any longer, I expelled it, which provided a fleeting moment of relief. Immediately following that, however, there came the sudden and overwhelming urge to take in another breath, one I could not ignore. Left with no other choice, I took a thick, lung-flooding breath of water. To my surprise, I felt no pain, nor the reflex to cough; I merely had the urge to exhale again. A rush of water left my lungs, and then again, I took a breath.

I felt a warm, peaceful feeling take over me, relaxing my limbs and easing my fearful thoughts. My eyes closed and the sea went silent, and it occurred to me that I had drowned.

What a shame, I thought. *Had I only known life was so short. . . .*

Chapter Nine

I sat forward in my seat with a desperate gasp, startling the old woman to my left so badly that she jumped and screamed. I jumped from my seat as well, still coughing imagined seawater from my lungs, my heart pummeling madly against my chest.

The young man to my right took me by one shoulder and eased me back into my seat. "Are you all right, miss?"

I nodded. The young man went to the old woman and helped her back to her seat.

"What was that all about?" asked the woman.

"I think she was having a nightmare, Madam."

I looked around the room, wondering if I might find some sign indicating whether my nightmare continued yet. I reasoned that the trauma of drowning had to have been enough to wake me, and yet I could not be certain. The previous dreams had been very lucid, indistinguishable from reality, in fact. There was nothing else to do but stay where I was and hope nothing else bizarre or terrifying happened while I waited for my stop. For some time, I didn't talk to anyone. I didn't *look* at anyone. I simply waited.

"Are you sure you're all right?" the young man asked, moving close enough to show his concern while remaining far enough to respect my personal space.

I turned to him and gave another smile and nod, but I must have been unimpressive in my delivery because he did not look at all convinced.

"Are you ill?" he asked.

"No."

"Do you need assistance of any kind?" he asked.

"No."

"Are you all right?"

I held my response.

He glanced away, looking lost in thought for a moment before turning back. "You know, I worked under a doctor for a short while, and I think I know of a treatment you might find helpful."

"I'm not interested."

"I have a friend who makes a patented tonic I think you might want to try." He pulled a small bottle from an inside jacket pocket. "It will relax you—and also works well against stomach upset, chronic cough, blurry vision, insomnia, body pain, and sexual dysfunction."

"Thank you, but I don't want your tonic."

He sat back, looking even more surprised than I had expected he would.

I crossed my arms, feeling indignant. I decided I would pretend he was no longer there, and then the frightful thought hit me that perhaps I was *still* dreaming and the man beside me was to be the next character to play in my nightmare.

I felt the palms of my hands go sweaty, and I rubbed them against my skirt to dry them. I waited quietly: I waited for a whale to swallow the train; I waited for some giant monster to burst through the window beside the old woman on my left; I waited for the man beside me to turn into the Bogey-Man and pull another knife to my throat. I waited for all these possibilities and more, but none came. My strange nightmare had come and gone. I was awake. I had nothing to fear. Still, I could not shake the uneasy feeling that still permeated through me, a feeling that something terrible was yet to come, something I felt sure would be the end of me if I were not prepared for it.

I lost all doubts that I might still be dreaming when the monotony of the train ride offered a dreadfulness all its own. The man on my right fell asleep and began to snore loudly. A woman two rows down felt the need to sing German folk songs, perhaps to drown out the snoring, and someone else made a horrific attempt at following along in harmony. I covered my ears, for the little that it helped. I tried to ignore him, but the endeavor was futile.

He suddenly had my full attention when I noticed the look on his face. It was as though he were witnessing something unforgettably grotesque, his closed eyes only adding to the intensity of his expression. I considered waking him, there being the added incentive of ending the sporadic bouts of snoring, but he spoke before I had the chance.

"I recognize him. Don't you?" he asked.

I watched his brow rise. He frowned deeply.

"Yes, that's him. I'm sure of it," he said. His lower lip trembled. "This is it, then."

I waited for him to say something more, but he pursed his lips before his face once again fell into a terrible grimace.

"How did you find me?" he asked.

I watched, my curiosity getting the best of me. I waited to see if he would say anything that might shed some light on the odd situation. Instead, he shook his head.

"No—please!" he cried.

I looked around. No one else seemed to notice the man's distress.

"No!" he continued.

I leaned toward him, trying to summon the courage to give him one quick nudge, but then I fell back as he flailed his arms in front of him. One of his hands caught me in the shoulder, and he woke with a surprised yowl. He blinked his eyes a few times and turned to me with an apologetic wince.

"I was having a nightmare," he said.

I nodded. "I could tell."

That seemed to satisfy him for the moment, but then he turned to me again with that concerned glare and asked, "Was I talking in my sleep?"

"A little."

"What did I say?"

I shrugged. "Nothing that made sense."

"Oh."

He sat back, going quiet again. After only a minute or two, he laughed aloud and turned back to me. "Our dream lives can be . . . nonsensical sometimes, don't you think?"

"I suppose."

An unexpected smile came to his face, but I realized it was an effect of the fear he obviously could not shake. "I keep dying."

"I beg your pardon?"

"In my nightmares," he said. "I keep dying in my nightmares."

I swallowed hard. "Oh?"

He shook his head and sat back once more. I was certain he had finished speaking; however, he turned to me again and said. "Have you ever seen Death in your dreams?"

"I can't say I have," I said as flashes of the masque dream jumped to the forefront of my mind.

He must have noticed the look of recognition because he gave me an inquisitive glare. "Never?"

I shrugged. "I don't know."

"You don't know?"

"No, I don't."

He shook his head. "Well, you're lucky then. Death is terrible."

I gave him a sideways glance then turned away completely.

"Don't you even want to know what he looks like?"

I shook my head.

"You're not curious?"

"I don't want to hear about your dream," I said.

"That's too bad," he said.

Something about his response struck me as strange. It wasn't so much what he said as the way he said it and the way he looked at me when he said it. "Too bad?" I had to ask.

"Too bad," he said.

"Would you care to elaborate?"

He shook his head. "Why should I?"

"Why do you think it's too bad?"

He rolled his eyes and laughed incredulously. "Why should you care?"

I thought about it for a moment, and then I shrugged back in my seat, feeling the fool. I realized that the only reason I did care was because he had implied some kind of vague importance to it. I had no more use for the images in his nightmares than I had for the images in my own. How I had allowed this man to rope me into his useless discourse suddenly was beyond me. I resolved to ignore him for the rest of the ride. He made it difficult at times, as he seemed unable to put an end to his boredom alone and attempted to draw me into further discussions.

Each time he brought up something new, my reply was the same: "Why should I care?"

The reply flustered him, and yet he continued to come back for more.

"I once saw an Ourang-Outang running wild down the streets."

"Why should I care?"

"I knew a man who said he saw an angel comprised of liquor bottles. Of course, I think he was drunk at the time, but—"

"Why should I *care?*"

"Have you ever heard the story about the inn at the harbor?"

"Why *should* I *care?*"

"Do you know it's quite rude to answer

continuously, 'Why should I care?'"

"*Why should I care?*"

"You are a most insufferable woman."

"*Why should I care?*"

Finally, he turned up his nose and veered away for good. He muttered just loud enough for me to be able to hear, "I thought you should know that I saw you in my nightmare."

I turned to him, but he refused to meet my glance.

I tried not to seem interested, reminding myself multiple times that a random stranger's bad dream was none of my concern regardless of whom he insisted he had seen in it. Chances were he was merely trying to reel me in for more time-wasting chatter. Still, the curiosity did eat at me and it took all of my will to keep from initiating further discourse on the matter. He seemed content to hold his silence, now that he supposedly had something to say, but I played his game through to the end of my ride and basked in the bittersweet silence.

By the time I finally reached Baltimore, I was so eager to make my distance with the train that I nearly forgot Neptune and my luggage. The hound was happy to see me, wagging his tail wildly even before I had him out of the crate. I found a ride to a nearby hotel, where I checked in at their weekly rate—then snuck Neptune in through a service stairwell. He moved along with me quietly, as if he knew exactly what was going on, and he calmly found a corner in which to nap as soon as I let him into the room.

I immediately set out to find Mr. Poe, but quickly learned that the task would not be so easy to complete. I knew he lived in Baltimore (at least he did according to Brantley's letter) but beyond that, I knew nothing. I had no street address, not even a street name. To make matters worse, no one I asked seemed to know who he was. I searched every street within my reach, but it seemed I had no way to reach him.

After nearly a week in Baltimore, it became evident to me that I would need to find some means of income if I was going to stay much longer. I wrote my family and explained my situation, hoping they might have something extra to spare. In the meanwhile, I looked around for work, although I found that there was very little available. Most of what I was able to apply for entailed scrubbing toilets or caring for some rich, lazy woman's child, so I was happy when I was able to land a position washing linen for the hotel that was housing me. The hours were long and the work tedious, but it gave me the freedom to search for Mr. Poe on evenings and weekends, while also affording me the means to remain in Baltimore until I had given the man his message. I searched through every route I could think of, looking in every kind of establishment. Either this man did not want to be found, or he simply did not exist.

I kept the letter in plain sight, rationalizing that if one of the maids decided to steal from my room, she would be more inclined to steal something hidden deep in a drawer than something left out. The letter remained untouched throughout my stay, although I did run up against a bit of unfortunate luck on another front.

Someone had discovered Neptune, despite his

perfect behavior, and suddenly I found myself without a home or a job. I had tried to plead my case—that I would pay extra for the dog and would see to it that he caused no damage—but the owner would not hear of any animals staying on the premises. Neptune and I spent a couple of nights sleeping in commercial porches and across park benches before finally I conceded my defeat.

"I tried my best," I told the dog. "It just wasn't good enough. It might be time to return to Norland."

He followed me as I wandered the streets in search of a ride to the nearest seaport. One carriage stopped for me, but quickly rode on when the driver saw the state of my dress and the hound at my side. I ran after it, brandishing a dollar bill to show I was good for the money, but it did not stop again. I stood in the center of the road, watching it continue into the distance, and I found myself fighting tears. Here I was, the homeless widow trying to survive without an ally in the world. I had nothing, no one to lean against, and my funds were waning quickly. I still had both wedding bands, but I would need those to get back across the sea.

Neptune stayed by my side as I made my way up the long street. Not one carriage passed us, not that one would have stopped had there been any to do so. My luck had been terrible since the move to New England, and I began to have the nagging feeling that this place *simply did not want me here*. I walked slowly, feeling the weight of my defeat.

I turned, and immediately I froze in place with a surprised gasp as I saw a woman frantically running away down the road. I would have ignored the woman, my distractions already plenty enough, had it not been for the fact that this woman held a peculiarly notable similarity to me. I could have thought the woman my twin had I not already known for certain that a twin did not exist.

"Hello!" I called out.

To my surprise, she quickened her pace.

I hurried after her, too stunned by her presence to think about what I was doing, and I lost her immediately after following her into a crowded pub.

Chapter Ten

As soon as I swung open the heavy door, a din of chatter flooded over me. Nearly every seat was taken and several people also stood, filling every pocket of empty space. It was dark and smoky inside, making it difficult to identify anyone without getting too close. I surveyed the room from the doorway, unsure whether I was willing to push through the crowds just for another chance to view my mysterious double. I tried telling myself that people see others with their likeness all the time, but then the image of her flashed through my mind and I shuddered. She did not hold my likeness, but my very face. When she moved, I saw my mannerisms and figure. It was as though I had seen me running away from myself.

Moved by her uncanny resemblance, I stepped further into the pub and began to sift through the sea of people. I moved from one table or group to the next, searching carefully for the woman, but she seemed to have vanished.

As I began to question my sanity, a young man approached me. He was tall and slender, and he wore an expensive suit with a gold-chained pocket watch. "Karina! Where have you been? I've been searching everywhere for you."

It came as a shock to hear the stranger utter my name. For reasons beyond me, however, I did my best to hide my confusion. "You have?"

I stepped back as he moved to embrace me. A puzzled look came to him as he allowed me my distance. "Is everything all right?" he asked.

I shook my head. "I'm not sure."

"But you seemed fine just minutes ago."

My hand went to my head, as if to dull some imaginary ache. "I did?"

"We were having a fantastic time. What happened?" he asked.

I looked down at my dirty, tattered skirt. "I'm not sure. There was a woman who looked just like me. I think she might be the woman you're looking for."

"We don't have time for these silly games," he said, taking my hand and pulling me toward a half-occupied table. "Could you please just *pretend* to like the Wilsons, at least until Will confirms the contract?"

A well-dressed couple, presumably the Wilsons, sat beside one another. They seemed happy to see my companion and me as we joined them across the table, but it was soon evident that their happiness was contrived. This was clearly a business meeting, any friendship between my companion and Mr. Wilson being purely superficial. It seemed strange that my group was so overdressed, and even stranger that they did not take notice of my ragged attire. That I knew no one there only magnified the uneasy feeling that churned through me, and the tension I could feel building across the table between all of us magnified it even greater.

"How is little Jack Junior getting along?" asked Mr. Wilson, addressing me.

I stared back at him for a few seconds, too stunned by the question to formulate an immediate answer. "Jack Junior? Oh, he's . . . well, you know Junior."

"He broke his arm, poor little boy," said my companion, whom I could deduce was Jack Senior.

I nodded my agreement.

"I'm sorry to hear that," Mrs. Wilson said. "Will and I will be sure to keep him in our prayers, won't we, darling?"

"Indeed," said Mr. Wilson.

"Please, I was hoping we might discuss the Poe account," said Jack.

I felt my stomach go tight at the sound of the man's name, and suddenly I had a dozen questions I wanted to ask. Mindful of Jack's position, whatever that was, I opted to save my questions for later and do my best to continue playing along.

Mr. Wilson nodded. "We probably should." He paused, looking reflective, then rubbed his tired eyes before continuing. "No one's been able to contact him. He's not receiving messages, not even answering his door."

"That is a problem," Jack said. "Might he finally have . . . you know?"

"Gone interminably mad? It is a distinct possibility," said Mr. Wilson.

Jack took a deep, slow breath. "He was ready to sign."

"I know how important this contract was, so I'll try to make it up to you somehow. I hear they're looking for *particularly gifted* masonry workers to work on a commercial property development here in town."

"My men and I would appreciate it."

"It's the least I can do. Now, if you'll excuse us, we have a gala to attend tonight." He and Mrs. Wilson stood in perfect unison. "You will hear from me by the end of the week, my friend—I promise!"

We watched the two make their exit. I gave Jack my most serious, inquisitive expression as I asked, "What was that all about?"

"Business. You know how it goes."

"Who is Mr. Poe?"

He glared at me with both concern and irritation. "I've only been telling you about his estate for two weeks now!" He scoffed. *"Who is Mr. Poe?"*

"Can you take me to his estate?" I asked.

"Why on earth would I want to do that?"

I considered telling him about the sealed letter, but I didn't want to risk the possibility that he would take it from me. I couldn't be sure why he behaved as though he knew me, but his concern seemed genuine. Moreover, he had known my name. Was it possible that my double was also named Karina?

"You're behaving strangely," he said. "Let me take you home."

We both stood, but I was hesitant to leave the table. I was not this man's Karina, and I couldn't simply leave with him and attempt to play the part, but I also couldn't part ways without learning Mr. Poe's whereabouts. Again, I searched the room for the other Karina, desperate to set things straight. Still, I saw no trace of her.

"Karina?"

I turned to him, my mind locked in a horrifying loop of wretched indecision. "This isn't right," I said, struggling to hold my composure.

He took my hand, but I snatched it away.

"Why are you making a scene?" he asked in an angry whisper.

I shook my head, too confused with this surreal new scenario to think any more about it. "I'm not well," I finally said. Truly, this case of mistaken identity had a light upset stirring in the pit of my stomach, threatening to grow into something more. I brushed past Jack and hurried to the door.

Upon exiting, I saw that Neptune no longer waited where I had left him. I cursed my haste in searching for the other Karina, revolted at the thought of him getting lost and becoming a stray. Jack came up behind me.

"What are you doing?" he asked.

"My dog, someone must have taken him," I said, my eyes still searching.

"Karina, we don't have a dog."

"You might not, but I do," I said, shrugging away as he tried to put a hand on my shoulder. I began to walk down the street.

He followed me. "Where are you going?"

"To find my dog."

"There is no dog!"

I stopped walking so I could turn to address him

properly. "I have two things I need to take care of: I need to find my dog and deliver a letter to Mr. Poe. If you want to help me—" I watched as my double hurried out of the pub and ran away in the opposite direction up the street. "There!" I pointed.

"No more games!" Jack said. He began to drag me across the street toward a carriage.

"There's your woman!" I yelled, doing my best to get him to turn around.

He was much stronger than I was, and thus he overpowered me quickly. He had me in the carriage in an instant, and then suddenly we were riding together into a residential area.

"You're making a mistake!" I tried.

"Whatever is the matter with you, my dear, the good Dr. Tarr will get to the bottom of it. I'll send for him as soon as we get home."

"You'll send for no one! I'm in town on personal business and I intend on conducting it!"

He shook his head, genuinely saddened by what he saw as the ranting of a woman gone mad. "You need rest. It's been a trying week for us both."

"Trying indeed!" I crossed my arms.

He placed his hand on my lap then squeezed my thigh as I moved to swipe it away. "You can't punish me forever, Karina."

"I'm not punishing you."

"Yes, you are. I know how you get when you're angry," he said.

I gave up trying to explain myself and spent the rest of the short ride sulking quietly. He seemed content with my silence, opting himself not to say anything more until we reached the house. We turned down a long, private road and my body shifted forward. I watched intently through the windshield as I caught a glimpse of the small estate up ahead.

The closer we drove, the worse condition I realized the two-story house was in. The garage and servant apartments both looked sealed off. One of the windows on the house's once impressive front had an enormous crack across it. The crack branched out across the glass in a way that created a rough, distorted image of a heart slowly breaking in two. It was a fitting welcome.

"Let's go inside, Karina."

I surveyed the remote area, already planning my escape. I knew I couldn't outrun his carriage, and because of that, I was trapped here until he turned his back on me or took me back to town. I decided it best to play his Karina until I could convince him I was well, then make my escape the next chance I could convince him to drive me back.

I let him escort me from the carriage to inside the home, where the nanny eagerly met us. She was unsightly thin and wore a standard uniform with her fiery hair pulled into one enormous bun.

"Little Jack has been calling for you all afternoon," the nanny said as she eyed my tattered dress.

"Has he?" I asked, having no desire to meet the child.

"Mrs. Allan is not feeling well, Constance. I'll need you to entertain Jack in the nursery," he answered, leading me upstairs.

"He's getting restless . . . and he's in need of reassurances from *both* of you," replied the nanny.

"You'll find a way to deal with him," he answered

back. He showed me down the upstairs hallway, almost as if he knew I needed showing around, and then opened the door at the end of the hall.

My hand clutched the threshold molding as I peered inside. The bed was fancy, but old and worn, the bedspread and pillows also appearing long used. There was a cedar chest at the foot of the bed and a matching dresser and writing desk against the adjacent wall.

"Why don't you take a nap?" Jack suggested.

I nodded. "I will. Thank you."

As I moved toward the bed, I heard the door shut behind me—then the *click* of a lock. I hurried to the door and tried it, only to find that it was indeed locked. I beat my hand against the door. "What is the meaning of this?"

"It's for your own good, Karina. I'm sending for Dr. Tarr right now. He'll know what to do."

I tugged on the doorknob then hit the door several times with an angry fist. "Unlock this door immediately!"

"You know I can't do that. I need to walk away now. I need to go send for Dr. Tarr."

"Don't you dare!" I peered through the keyhole, desperation hitting me as he indeed began to walk away. After only a few seconds, all I could see was the long, dark, empty hall.

"I'll be back soon, my rose."

"Unlock this door!"

He did not reply.

"Let me out of here!" I pounded and kicked upon the door in an attempt to beat it down, but the wood was thick and the threshold sturdy enough to withstand my blows. I suddenly felt as though I were in a coffin of a new sort. It had more room and a little more sunlight, but it was stifling, lonely, and cold just the same.

Giving up on the door, I moved to the window for some other means of escape. There seemed to be no safe passage down, the window leading only to a straight, two-story drop into the garden. Upon closer inspection, I saw that the window had been nailed shut, so even if there were a means down, I still did not have the means to get to it. I looked out over the vast garden filled with dead rose bushes and rotting trellises, wondering how I was going to manage my way out of this questionable captivity. I wondered if this was not the first time that door had locked in a hapless guest, my plight too odd to be some mere coincidence . . . and was there a connection between my kidnapping and my search for Mr. Poe?

I heard the faint cry of a young child and returned to the door to listen.

"I want my momma!" cried the little boy.

"Your momma is sleeping right now, and if you wake her up, you're going to get a whipping!" warned the nanny in a hushed voice.

I hit the door again. "Hello? Could you come here, please?"

"Now you've done it! Back to the nursery with you!" said the nanny, prompting an immediate screech from the child. "Back you go!"

"No—come *here!*" I yelled. "I want to talk to you!"

Everything went eerily quiet. I listened carefully, my ear against the door, but no one made a sound.

"Hello? Are you out there?" I yelled, hitting the hard, heavy wood once more. No one was listening. Thoughts of my seaside coffin by the lighthouse came to mind: the horror of being trapped in my own clothing chest; the desperate hours I spent trying to scratch my way out, the weight of the sand holding me fast; the smell of brine, flounder, and cedar in the thinning air. . . .

The smell of the cedar in the room became overwhelming. I felt an uneasy heaviness to my lungs as my mind replayed Brantley's attempted murder. I felt the attack as if it were happening all over again, and then I felt that same pang of emptiness I had first felt when I woke a half meter beneath the tide fronts in that awful makeshift casket.

"Help! Let me out!" I screeched.

No one heard me.

My resolve weakening, I moved to the bed and sat down. It was comfortable despite its aged appearance, but there was no way I could relax with the door locked like that.

I wondered how long he intended on keeping me there, and I felt another wash of panic as I considered the plans Jack might have in mind for me. I searched the room for a possible weapon, noting the table lamp; however, I went to lift it from the desk only to find that it was fixed securely to the wood.

I searched the dresser drawers, but they were filled strictly with articles of clothing. I moved to the cedar chest, but it was locked and I had no possession of a key. I sat down on the smooth wooden surface, too mentally exhausted to try to make any further sense of what I was doing there or how I might get away. I would stay there until I could convince Jack to lengthen the leash, and then I would find some means to encourage him to lengthen it a little more. I would need to remain calm if I was going to win over the man's confidence, and so calm I resolved to be. My heart began to pound hard and fast despite me when I heard someone approach the end of the hall.

Chapter Eleven

I waited in the far end of the room as the door unlocked, then opened. I cowered beside the writing desk as Jack entered with a man in a white doctor's coat.

The man had curly dark hair and Mediterranean features. He wore an expensive suit beneath his coat and carried a large, black bag that jingled with the clink of multiple vials and bottles hitting one another as he moved.

Jack closed the door and stood by it. "Dr. Tarr is here to help."

"Your husband told me all about what's going on, Mrs. Allan," said the doctor. "Why don't you also tell me . . . in your own words?"

"My husband has gone mad," I said.

"He told me you had said he was confusing you with another woman, another woman who happened to look exactly like you and *also* answered to Karina. Is that true?" asked Dr. Tarr.

"He's keeping me locked in this dark, tiny room,"

I replied. "I would like assistance in escaping this house immediately."

Jack gave the doctor a horrified glance. "She underwent a sudden shift during a casual business meeting with my boss and his wife. It was. . . ." He went quiet for a moment, a look of recognition flashing across his face. He turned back to me. "It was when we started discussing the account with Mr. Poe. How do you know him, Karina?"

"I don't know him."

Jack gave the doctor a subtle nod, prompting him to set down his bag and open it. I watched with nowhere to go and no means of defense as Dr. Tarr pulled two bottles and a small measuring spoon from the bag.

"What are you doing?" I asked.

"I'm just putting together a little something to help you relax," said Dr. Tarr.

"I don't want it."

The doctor moved toward me with a dull, cloudy concoction. There was no more than a teaspoon or two of it, and yet something about even that looked powerful and threatening. "It's for your own good. It will make you feel much better."

I refused the spoon.

"Mrs. Allan, I would like to do what I can to prevent your madness from taking full hold."

"*My* madness?"

"If you should refuse my help, and should your husband complain that you have become unmanageable and of further danger to the child—"

"Further danger?"

"—I'll have no choice but to send you for

treatment at an asylum instead."

"An asylum?"

"Just drink Dr. Tarr's medicine," Jack interjected.

"An *asylum*?"

The doctor extended the spoon again. "It's perfectly safe."

I stared at the terrible liquid, unwilling to take it.

"Please, Mrs. Allan, we can do this the easy way or the hard way—and I don't think you'd like the hard way." He gave me a stern look that told me he was serious.

I took the spoon and hesitantly raised it to my lips, but then paused once more.

"Do this—for me if not for yourself," Jack said.

The doctor nodded.

I allowed the bitter liquid to rush into my mouth then swallowed it quickly. A sudden warmth saturated my body, and then a slow but steadily increasing sense of relaxation weakened my muscles.

"Was that so hard?" asked Dr. Tarr. He met Jack at the door and showed him the bottles and measurements. "Give her a teaspoon every four hours and send for me when she finishes the bottle."

The terrifying shock of being drugged for an extended period hit me, but the fear dissolved almost immediately, as did all of my other cares, when an incredible, blissful abandon took over. I stumbled back, falling against the bed. I lay against the soft bedspread, realizing that I could not will my limbs to lift me from my spot. I no longer cared about my captivity as I succumbed to the intense desire to close my eyes and rest for a while.

I heard the door shut and lock, but that was all

right. In my mind's eye, I stood by the ocean, watching the waves crashing nearby. It was either sunrise or sunset, the water glimmering with the ever-changing colors of the horizon. Seagulls congregated near the tide, fighting over small fish. I took a deep breath and savored the salty sea air.

I had always loved the ocean, dangerous and scary as it could be. As a child, I couldn't see enough of the beach. It brought me a sense of calm I could not easily describe. Very little could compare to the feeling that came with sitting at the seaside, watching one wave crash after the next as the warm sun beat down and filtered against the tide's misty spray.

Like a dream, I moved along the shore, taking in all of the wonderful sights, sounds, and smells. I turned toward a rocky cliff side that overlooked the breakers. The waves were entrancing, the colors dazzling against the painted sky.

"Karina, my rose," a distant voice echoed.

A hint of rose dashed across the sky and shimmered in the crashing waves. I leaned forward, looking directly below. The breaking waves toppled and arched over one another before hitting the heavily eroded wall of rock and shellfish. I stood a dizzying height over the tumultuous water, wondering how deep the surface fell. I knew I would drown even if I survived any potential impact, and yet I jumped.

"Karina, can you hear me?" I heard a ghostly familiar voice ask as I plunged into the frigid water.

"*Maelström!*" I heard another voice cry out from some other unknown depth.

The cold water rushed all around me. I thought to look up, and I noted hints of sunlight coming in through the surface far above. I began to kick and grab toward the surface, but I continued to sink. A peculiar sensation came over me as the air began to escape my fighting lungs.

This has happened to me before.

I labored to find the connection, the memory that fit, but I could not. I realized that the waking dream induced by the drug had to be drawing upon past dreams as well as real memories, allowing my mind to become confused between the two. My perceptions were no more real than a dream created through actual sleep, and this dream would likely last until the drug I'd ingested had run its course.

I felt a hand grasp mine, then the firm but gentle tug of my body being pulled through the water. I felt the cold air as it hit my skin, the gritty sand as my body dragged along the beach, then the warmth of Brantley's lips against mine as he forced his breath into my lungs.

I turned aside and coughed the water from my lungs, my body nearly too weak to move.

"What were you doing?" Brantley asked.

I looked around, a terrible chill racing through me as I saw the lighthouse nearby.

"You nearly drowned," he continued, his voice hinting that either he was worried or terribly angry.

"How did I get here?" I asked.

"You must have been somnambulating again, my love."

I shook my head, too confused to answer immediately. "Somnambulating? Here?"

"It is fortunate that I happened to roll over and notice you were gone."

"This isn't right," I said, and suddenly every sense of delineation I had held between reality and dream fell into the crashing waves beside us. Wasn't Brantley dead? I had thought so. How had I gotten to the ocean? I had been locked away in the furthest reaches of a lunatic's house. Had the drugs he forced me to drink taken me so far from all that was real?

"I'm so glad I found you in time," Brantley said, resting in the sand beside me.

"You aren't here," I tried.

He slid his body over mine so that our chests and stomachs met. "No?"

I shook my head.

"Whatever is haunting you, it was just a terrible nightmare," he said. "You can relax now. It's over and I'm here."

Although I wanted to believe, I knew it was all merely an illusion within my mind. The thought that Brantley had never crossed me, that we were happy together, was an enticing one. I felt my mind ease into the fantasy, my soul too empty for me to deny myself a moment of happiness. I closed my eyes as he kissed me, his body moving with a level of passion I had not seen in him for some time. I gave in to the advance, unable to resist him. His touch felt so good. Too good.

"This is a dream," I said as he tore away and discarded, one by one, the layers beneath my heavy skirt.

"Is it?" he asked before kissing me again.

His lips were soft, his beard unmistakable. No, he was dead. This was happening only within the confines of my own intoxicated mind. As real as it felt, it was nothing but a devious trick. I told myself I would not let myself fall into it, and then suddenly his unique, musky scent hit me and I felt helpless to his embrace.

The water crashed in just to our side as we kissed and caressed one another. He shed his clothes as quickly as he had torn away mine, and our bodies came together, speaking their silent language, shifting into one in movement and in soul. He had been my betrothed, my one and only, my finger still tightly bound by the ring that held us together.

"Don't ever forget this moment," he said, taking me with as much graceful force as he could.

The tide reached in just a little further, sending a cool rush over our hot, thrashing bodies.

"Why?" I asked.

"It will serve to remind you who is the master and who is the bitch," he said, suddenly driving against me forcefully.

"I don't understand," I said, my muscles unresponsive as I tried to break away from him.

"You belong to me," he said, his sudden shift turning my pleasure into pain.

The tide came in even higher, threatening to cover me completely. I coughed and writhed as water washed over my face just high enough to send light streams down my nose and mouth. I gasped and choked, struggling to breathe as Brantley continued with selfish fervor, then I took a quick and heavy gulp of air as I realized that there was no water.

I opened my eyes, surprised to find myself on the bed in the locked room with Jack on top of my nearly paralyzed body. There was nothing I could do to slow his painfully greedy pace, so I lay there and endured it until he was finished with me. I felt raw and dirty as he left, the click of the lock telling me that it mattered not how I had found my way there; I was trapped in this spider's web, his venom holding me paralyzed, unable to defend myself against its dark advances. It didn't matter who this man was. What mattered now was what he had become to me.

I realized my mind was beginning to clear, and also that I had regained use of my limbs. Tired and weak, I sat up, searched for my dress, and put it on. I moved barefooted to the door. I glanced out the keyhole, but the hall was empty. I tried the door. It was locked.

I began to pace the room, the combination of nerves and fatigue beginning to get the best of me. My emotions took hold and I gave into the temptation to cry. My hands slowly clenched as I staggered back and forth, my lungs heaving and my soul moaning. I knew my sanity would crumble for good if I did not find a way out soon.

I returned to the window, wondering if I might break the glass and somehow find my way down to safety. I searched for a possible makeshift ladder, but the room contained nothing I could use. There were not enough bedcovers to tie together for a rope, and everything else was nailed down. Jumping was out of the question.

A spark of hope hit me as I saw the nanny and the little boy enter the garden together. The boy looked to be around three or so, and he had wispy blond hair all about his head. He bent down to pick up and examine rocks and sticks, mindful of the cast and wrap that bound his right arm to his chest. The nanny stayed by his side, patiently allowing the boy to explore the various sights and textures nature had to share.

I knocked on the glass, and the nanny looked up at me.

I leaned against the window. "I'm locked in!"

She watched me for a moment, her face flat and unresponsive, and then she turned back to the boy and ushered him from my view. I tried to gain her attention again, but with no luck. It seemed she had no intention of helping me.

I shifted my attention elsewhere, watching instead the waning light and the shadows growing all across the garden. The sun was slowly on its way out. Soon, night would fall. Soon, the room would be dark, very dark. I watched the sky begin to change color, the cloudy blue slowly being swallowed by swatches of purples and pinks. The twilight seemed almost unreal, my view through the window seemingly a painting through the glass. Everything was deathly still.

I turned around with a surprised gasp as the door unlocked and Jack entered with a covered food tray.

"You need to eat," he said, removing the metal lid.

I leaned forward as the sight and smell of chicken and dumpling stew hit my senses. Still, everything in me warned of the high possibility that more of the drug lay somewhere within my meal.

"Have a bite," I told him, my distrust evident.

He took a spoonful of chicken and broth and ate it without hesitation.

"Now, have a dumpling."

"What is this game you're playing?" he asked. He set the spoon in the bowl, but whether his agitation stemmed from frustration or guilt, I could not tell.

"You would call this a game?" I asked.

"What else would you call it?"

I thought to go to the door, but was too afraid to make the move. He set the tray on the desk and began his retreat. "Eat your supper," he said as he took hold of the doorknob and closed me back in. I heard the key engage the lock, and once more, I was alone in the ever-darkening room.

I used the last of my light to examine more carefully the bowl of stew. I tore apart one of the dumplings and sampled it with the tip of my spoon. Sure enough, the dumpling was bitter, clearly containing another dose of the drug. I rejected the entire meal just to be safe, although I knew he would expect me to take another dose one way or another. I moved to the foot of the bed and lifted the mattress, then I quickly scooped the stew onto the bed's wooden frame and dropped the mattress to conceal it. I set the bowl back onto the tray, praying he would not discover my trick.

I pretended to sleep when I heard him return. I moved not a hair as he quietly made his way across the room by the light of the lamp he carried. He shifted his key ring to the hand with the lamp then picked up the tray with his free hand and left. I heard the door awkwardly close behind him, but I did not hear the key turn the lock. When I felt sure he had left, I hurried to the door to look out the keyhole. It was dim, but I was still able to see that the hallway was empty.

Slowly, quietly, I tried the doorknob and held my breath as I pulled open the door. I carefully closed it behind me and began down the hall. I froze as a floorboard creaked beneath my foot. My heart began to race, my breaths each struggling to escape me as I stood perfectly still, listening for a sign that I had been detected. Hearing nothing, I continued toward the end of the hall and looked around the corner. Seeing no one, I continued to the staircase.

My heart sped even faster as I took the first step down. I felt certain he would appear from one of the downstairs rooms at any moment and snatch me back from my escape. My breaths seemed intent on giving me away, wheezing and desperate to release a distressed cry. I did my best to stay quiet, straining against each shaky breath to keep it slow and steady as I moved down to the next step, and then the next. I listened carefully as my ears picked up an argument occurring behind a closed door downstairs. I could not tell what they were arguing about, but I could tell from the tones they used that the argument was heated.

Deciding that I best make use of the distraction, I hurried down the stairs as quietly as I could and fled through the front door.

Chapter Twelve

I ran as fast as I could into the heavily wooded area that bordered the property, doing my best to keep view of the road that would eventually lead me back into town. The journey was notably slower by foot, especially given that mine were bare, but I was determined to put as much distance as I possibly could between me and the house before Mr. Allan noticed his most prized possession was not there. I knew he would seek me out immediately, and perhaps he would even collect a small team of friends to search the woods, so it was imperative that I found somewhere to hide quickly.

Much to my relief, I encountered no one in the forest. The misty, early evening air was biting, but it was bearable as long as I kept moving. My dress did nothing to help, the fabric too light to block out the elements. I held at a brisk pace, fearing numbness in my extremities should I dare slow my pace. I covered as much ground as I could until dusk gave way to the dark, and the sudden threat of running face-first into a tree had me feeling my way through the dense woods at a guarded walk.

I waited to hear Jack's carriage come up the road nearby, just as I waited to hear the call of helping friends. I considered the possibility that one or more of those friends could have hounds trained to track. I listened for their howling barks, but my ears picked up nothing save the sound of my feet moving across the pine needles layered lightly over the tightly packed earth. I watched for the light of lanterns, relieved when I did not see any.

I considered that Jack may have decided to leave me be for the night, or at least until he decided I needed another dose of the doctor's mind and body numbing concoction. If that were the case, I might actually make it to town and find a safe place to wait out the night. My first thought was to return to the train station and buy a ticket to the port where Brantley and I had arrived from Norland. I wanted to give my search for Mr. Poe one last try, but the thought of it left me uneasy. I had traveled across the region, been taken captive and drugged, then treated like a rag doll fit to take without defense a strange man's violent, licentious assault, and all for what? What was so important in that letter that I should endure such things?

I felt for the letter in my front pocket, finding it intact and secure beside Brantley's wedding band, and I resolved that I would break the seal and read the document as soon as I found a safe enough place and adequate light. I was certain the letter was about whatever legend or treasure Brantley had been led to believe was there, but the thought also crossed my mind that the letter might be some sort of confession. If that were the case, he might have implicated me as well. Of course, I could not allow such a thing to happen. I was a Lady of Norland after all, and as such, I had a certain reputation I needed to uphold.

My body ached and my feet were raw by the time I finally reached town, but I reached it without incident. No one searched for me. The streets were actually very quiet, which surprised me given the location and my estimate of the time. I searched for an open inn, but the only one I could find had a large "No Vacancy" sign on the door. I needed a good bath and a warm bed, but I would have settled for a blanket and a cot.

As I moved down the street, I noticed that every building had its shutters closed and none of the evening lamps were lit. I wondered if perhaps someone had seen signs of a terrible storm, although the slightly cloudy sky looked calm and I felt no wind. I turned a corner, only to see more of the same. Shutters covered every window. Every door was closed. No lamps burned. Nothing, not even a stray cat, stirred. I felt a surge of fear move through me as I realized whatever danger the town had felt the need to protect itself against, I was locked out with it.

Fog slowly rolled in, nearly imperceptible at first, but soon thick enough to obscure the tops of houses and creating a layer of haze all around me. It made the air feel icy and wet, and my body shivered beyond my control. I searched each building for a sign that I might enter, but the night's darkness matched with the fog made seeing difficult.

I turned with a jump as I heard a most unspeakable

sound. It was like a cry, only deep and animalistic. Whatever uttered it was large. I couldn't see anything, and that made the sound even more menacing. Muffled through the fog, it echoed from all around and I couldn't discern its specific source. I listened intently, and after only a moment, I heard a distinct chattering. I realized almost immediately that the chattering was of my own teeth, and I held my hand to my jaw to silence myself; however, I was too cold to be silent. My breaths escaped me in labored thrusts. I dragged my burning, swollen feet along the dusty road. I knew I needed to find shelter soon, lest I freeze to death before any other threat could find me. All the same, I went breathless and still when I heard the creature's deep shriek once more.

I held to the side of the street, vigilant and distraught, nearly ready to start pounding on a stranger's door. In my condition, I would likely be mistaken for a beggar, but I was running out of options.

A stable came into view, and again I heard the sound. This time, however, I realized that it was not the cry of some monster in the fog, but the *neigh* of a cold and restless horse. The service door was slightly ajar, but probably still open enough to let the chill into the stables.

One of the horses gave a jolted cry, spooked by my entrance. I closed the door behind me and near blackness suddenly filled the stable, making my presence all the more threatening to the animals. They stirred about in their stalls, so I stood by the door until they calmed. When they finally did, I began to search for a clean corner to huddle against and was grateful to find a pile of straw for cover. I piled the straw over my body, burying myself in it. The warmth it afforded me was not substantial yet ample enough to keep me from freezing.

I closed my eyes, but despite my fatigue, sleep did not come. I couldn't stop thinking about the empty streets and closed shutters, the fog, and the man who would be tracking me by morning. A nearby horse whinnied occasionally, and each time I peeked from the straw in anticipation of something to come. I tried to make out what I could of the street through the spaces between the wooden planks, but all I could see was one foggy shadow after another. I couldn't shake the feeling that I was terribly unsafe, that someone (or something) was out there searching the streets for me—or for someone like me.

I thought I heard a snarl come somewhere outside, but with the wind suddenly picking up, it was hard to tell. The horses began to exchange nervous sounds, so I scurried to submerge myself completely in the hay.

I jumped as something hit the side of the building with an abrupt *thud*.

The horses moved restlessly about their stalls, voicing their distress. I stayed where I was, holding as still as I could as someone approached the service door and thin streaks of light from a lantern shone in between the wooden planks. I held my breath and closed my eyes, hoping for the best as the door opened and someone stepped inside. The person wore boots with heavy heels that made a distinctly loud sound against the ground. I heard the rhythmic clang of some kind of metal . . . but the sound was not made by keys, or jewelry, or anything else I could identify. Curious as I was to know what it was, I dared not move to look.

The door opened again and a second set of footsteps crossed inside. I heard a brief exchange.

"Are you sure no one followed you?" asked the loud-heeled man.

"No," answered the second man.

"Do you have the money?"

"Of course."

"This isn't what we agreed upon," said the loud-heeled man.

"Half now and half after it's done," said the second man.

"How do I know you're good for the rest of it?"

The second man laughed nervously. "Who in his right mind tries to cheat a killer for hire?"

"Keep it down, will you?"

"No one's out there—everyone closed up for the cold."

"Just keep it down. I've got a certain level of secrecy I have to keep if I'm going to run a business, if you get what I mean. Now, how do you want this man, this Mr. Poe, done?"

As I heard the name once more, I felt a shiver threaten to unveil my cover. I bit my tongue, knowing I would surely die a terrible death if I allowed my presence to be revealed to the men.

"I want it to look like an accident so there's no way they can trace it back to me," said the second man.

"Poison, maybe?"

"As long as it looks natural."

"Very good, then," said the loud-heeled man. He began toward the door. "I'll send word to you when I'm finished."

"And when do you think will that be?"

"Days . . . a week, perhaps. A job like this one takes planning. Do not contact me again. Do you understand?"

"Yes, sir."

The door opened and the loud-heeled man exited. The second man waited a few minutes before exiting as well, leaving the door just slightly ajar. I would have moved to close it had I not been so paralyzed by the conversation I had just secretly witnessed. The foggy air drifted in and again I shivered, but I waited until there was no possible way either man remained anywhere near enough to hear me before I found the courage to move from my hiding spot and shut the door. I hurried back to my hay pile and scampered beneath it, hoping that if one of them had happened to have heard me and returned to investigate, I might be fortunate enough to elude him a second time.

I wondered why someone would want to have, of all people, Mr. Poe poisoned, but I knew I needed to disown the affair. I had no idea where Mr. Poe was. Moreover, I didn't even know the man. For all I knew, he was one of the despicable swindlers responsible for our fateful move to the lighthouse. With Brantley's horrifying obsession with the place before his terrible end, it was only reasonable that the letter would be addressed to someone who had played a part in his securing the position there.

The question of what Brantley had to say to the man became consuming, but I had no light at the moment by which to read the letter and ease my curiosity. Brantley had not left any word to be sent back to Norland, not even a letter for his mother, whom he loved dearly and had hated to leave behind. Yet, he had a letter for a man about whom I had never heard any mention before the moment I discovered it. None of it made any sense.

My mind too active to allow me any sleep, I huddled in the hay and watched the rest of the night pass. As the first hints of day broke in through the cracks along the walls, the horses stirred and the ones in the nearest stalls began to take notice of me. They made an array of awful vocalizations while they stomped the ground with their hooves and hit the dividers with their flanks, effectively driving me from the building.

As I stepped out, a stable hand confronted me at the door and blocked my exit. He was a thin, dark man with grey eyes and ragged clothes. A large bucket of feed dangled from each hand. He eyed me angrily. "This is private property, Ma'am."

"I'm sorry. I was just leaving."

He set down the buckets. "We don't much like trespassers here. The stable master might want to have a word with you."

"I just needed to escape the cold. I had no other place to go. I didn't mean anyone any harm."

As he eyed my frayed dress, my unwashed face, and my tousled hair, a look of understanding crept over him. "It did fall below freezing last night."

"Please just let me leave," I said. "I swear I'm just passing through."

He took a deep breath, seemingly taking a moment

to confirm the decision in his mind. He nodded, moving from the door. "Go—but if I ever see you here again, you will speak to the proper authorities."

"Thank you!" I said, repeating the words twice over before running off.

I found my way to the port and even found a ship preparing to leave for Norland, only to learn that I hadn't nearly the funds to buy my pass. I offered the ticket man both of my wedding bands for passage, but he refused to barter, insisting they accepted money only, and directed me to a merchant in town who would likely perform the trade.

The ticket man's directions led me to a familiar street. I hurried as I passed the pub Jack had kidnapped me from, as though he might emerge from the building and drag me away from it once more. Just as I cleared the building, I saw the other Karina again. She walked up from the far end of the street with Neptune at her side. I thought to confront her, to take back my dog and find out what purpose she had playing my person, when I saw Jack behind her, even further down the road. I turned and ran, scrambling inside the closest building to me: the pub.

I hurried through the drunken crowd to the rear of the establishment, making the quick decision to hide as I came across an open closet. Standing amongst a dirty mop bucket, a toolbox, and used linen, I shut the door unnoticed, leaving it just open enough for me to peek out.

I saw my impostor enter, stop at the landing for a moment, and then begin to sift through the crowd. Jack entered a moment later, found her immediately, and dragged her out. I felt my breath go still for a moment, my fists clenching and my jaw going tight, as I worked up the courage to leave my hiding spot. I slipped out and mixed back into the crowd, still too shaken to return to my search for the gold merchant.

After a short while, Mr. and Mrs. Wilson entered and began to search for a table. I hid behind a standing crowd as the two approached another man. The three claimed a table as another party left, and curiosity moved me within earshot as they finished exchanging formal greetings and pleasantries.

"So, Mr. Poe," Mr. Wilson began. "I trust you have had enough time to consider my proposal?"

I felt myself gasp. So, this is Mr. Poe? I studied the man's troubled face, his dark, curly hair and matching moustache. He seemed . . . small for all of the attention he seemed to attract. I wondered what he could possibly be doing with the Wilsons, given that the businessman had previously suggested whatever arrangement they'd had with Mr. Poe had fallen through.

"I'm not yet convinced you have my best interests in mind," said Mr. Poe. He flagged down the barmaid as she neared them. "An ale, my dear."

"Make that two and put them both on my tab," Mr. Wilson said.

The girl nodded and hurried off. The men both waited quietly as the barmaid brought their ales.

Mr. Wilson took a swig from his cup before asking, "What makes you think I don't have your best interests in mind?"

"Well, to begin, you don't even consider the best interests of one of your men. This deal will obviously take away a good job I personally saw you promise him."

Mr. Wilson took another drink of ale. "I never promised him anything."

"Didn't you?" asked Mr. Poe.

"He has work elsewhere."

"Really? Another job that big?"

"Another private firm," said Mr. Wilson.

"Well, then." Mr. Poe took a single sip of his ale before standing. "I will be seeking my business elsewhere." He gave Mrs. Wilson a cordial bow then turned and walked out.

Mr. and Mrs. Wilson immediately began to argue, and I opted to hurry out while the two were thoroughly distracted. Neptune greeted me as I stepped outside. Delighted with the reunion, I bade him to follow me as I hurried to catch Mr. Poe.

Chapter Thirteen

He noticed me after we cleared only a few buildings, my hurried feet against the ground giving me away. He yelled without turning back, "I already told you we were through!"

"Mr. Poe, I need to speak to you," I called back, still trying to catch up with him.

"Whatever it is, I'm not interested!" he yelled, holding his quick pace.

"Please—I've traveled a long way to see you."

"You're a fan of my work then?"

"No, Mr. Poe, I'm afraid I've never heard of your work."

"So you're interested in the apartment? You need to make an appointment like everyone else," he said, his voice nearly falling into a growl.

"Apartment? I don't know what you're talking about."

He shook his head. "Please leave me be, Madam. I've had a trying day."

"Did you know a man named Brantley Reynolds?"

"I'm sorry, but I do not."

"What about the Burnswatch Lighthouse?"

He stopped, turning only enough to give me a sideways glance as I stopped just short of him. "What about that place?"

"I was hoping you might tell me why my husband left a letter for you before he hanged himself in the stairwell," I said, my throat going tight.

"How strange," he said and scratched his head. He turned back and continued to walk, but at a pace of which I was able to keep up.

"That's all you have to say about it?" I asked.

He shrugged. "What does the letter say?"

"I haven't opened it."

"You have come to deliver it then?"

"We have more than just the letter to discuss," I said, a newfound sense of vigilance taking over me as I recalled the conversation I had overheard the previous night. "Is there somewhere we might talk in private?"

"If you don't mind walking a little further, we're nearly there. You must pick up your pace though. I fear someone might be following us," he said.

I looked behind me and all around, but I did not see anyone.

"Quick!" he said, turning down another road. It was heavily rutted with patches of farmland and rural housing on one side and short stretches of apartments and small storefronts on the other.

He began to run and I felt certain I was going to lose him. He turned again, and I caught a quick glimpse of him turning another corner just as I cleared the first. "Wait!" I yelled.

I turned the second corner in time to see him cross into a large public garden. Enclosed by white picket fences and vine-covered trellises, the garden contained several rose bushes and topiaries, all which surrounded an intimidating hedge maze. Neptune froze at the entrance, refusing to go in. I had no choice but to keep going, lest I lose Mr. Poe forever. As I cleared the trellis, a light panic fell upon me at the sight of Mr. Poe entering the maze. I followed apprehensively, afraid I might get lost, but then I realized that I was already lost. What was a hedge maze compared to the vast web of American streets?

I caught a glimpse of him as he made his first turn, and my stomach went tight as I struggled to stay on his tail. "Slow down!" I yelled, but he did not respond to me.

I tried to push my legs to move even faster through the quick turns and twists, but the strain did nothing to improve my speed. I stumbled over a rock and flew forward, toppling to the ground. I staggered to my feet and pushed forward, but already I had lost him.

"Mr. Poe!" I called out.

I heard nothing, not even the sound of other feet tapping against the tightly packed dirt of the maze floor. Deciding that Mr. Poe had been intent on losing me there, I decided to try my best to backtrack out. I was not going to pursue a man who did not want to be pursued, even with the information I had for him.

It only took me a moment to realize that I had forgotten the path. I began to choose directions blindly, my heart racing as the narrow walls of thick shrubbery seemed to lean in on me, towering, closing me in. I felt my chest go heavy, like my air was growing thin despite the open sky above me, and every breath seemed to grow more burdensome at the next turn. Every direction looked the same. There was no sign of the exit.

"Mr. Poe, if you can hear me, you've thoroughly succeeded in terrifying a dear young woman," I cried. "I cannot find the exit!"

"That's because you're nearly at the center," he called back from not too far away.

I followed the voice, finding Mr. Poe sitting on a bench in a small central courtyard. He looked up at me, and by his face I could tell he felt bad over the trick. I wiped away a couple of menacing tears and sat down on the other end of his bench.

"I had to ensure that we had lost them . . . and that you are not another one of the Englishman's spies," he said.

"An Englishman's spy!" I scoffed. I pulled the letter from my pocket. "This is what brought me here—this letter, written by my deceased husband! Do you even care what I had to go through, a penniless widow, to find you?"

He shook his head. "I'm terribly sorry," he said as he reached for the letter.

I snatched it back. "I'll give it to you—once I've had a chance to look at it myself."

He crossed his arms and went still, watching intently as I removed the wax seal and unfolded the letter. I looked over the document, which seemed to consist solely of three diary entries. I shook my head as I attempted to make sense of it.

I angled the print so Mr. Poe could see just as well. "Do you have any idea why he would want you to have this?"

He shook his head, scooting closer to get a better look.

The three entries mentioned the lighthouse, an exaggerated description of Brantley's "noble" standing, Neptune, and a vague hint of his goal of finding something priceless hidden there. Strangely, they made no mention of me, as if I had not been there at all. He even mentioned the rum, but gave no word about me traveling through the forest to get it for him.

"This is the entire document?" asked Mr. Poe, still clearly just as puzzled as I was.

I nodded.

He lifted the letter so he could look at the back, where his name and city were both written clearly in Brantley's shaky hand.

"I've never met your husband," said Mr. Poe, taking a moment to reflect before adding, "but you might find it interesting to know I have been researching the local legends surrounding the Burnswatch lighthouse."

"There's more than one?" I asked.

"Well," he began, his eyes shifting as he listened for any potential passers-by, "they say the place is cursed."

"I've heard that," I said, not impressed.

"There's a story for every person who has set foot in that place," he continued. "Some caretakers have reported nothing unusual at all . . . but so many more of them have died in so many hideous ways, each of their stories becoming a legend in one or more local areas."

"And you're not afraid I could be harboring a curse too?" I asked.

"There would be far too much irony in my demise becoming part of such a collection of legends," he said. "Besides, I'm living with far too many demons for my end to come so easily."

I sifted once more through Brantley's three entries, deciding finally that they were useless. I handed the document to Mr. Poe, who folded it and slid it into an interior coat pocket. He stood, looking ready to leave.

"About that," I said, feeling hesitant. "I overheard something last night . . . something you probably should know." I paused, feeling my own sense of concern over the possibility of eavesdroppers nearby.

"Yes?" he asked.

I took a deep breath. "Someone has hired a man to poison you."

"Do you know who?"

I shook my head.

"Did you hear anything else? Anything more specific?"

"Nothing else," I said. "I'm sorry."

He nodded cordially. "Thank you for the information, Madam. I shall take it to heart." He moved to enter back into the maze.

I jumped to my feet to follow him. "Please don't leave me in here!"

He sighed. "Very well. I'll show you out."

He kept a slow pace as he moved by memory through the winding passages, taking me through the backside of the maze. When we emerged, I noticed that we were on the opposite side of the park. Neptune spotted us and hurried to my side as I followed Mr. Poe to the park's exit.

"Don't you have somewhere to be going *other than where I'm going?*" he asked.

I shrugged, realizing it was time for me to consider again my passage back to Norland. "Do you know where the gold merchant is from here?"

He shook his head. "I don't have much use for gold."

"I need to trade my wedding bands for money so I can afford the boat ride home," I said.

"I'm sorry, but I don't know where your gold merchant is."

He crossed down another street and I followed.

"I'll kindly ask you to find your own way from here," he said as we neared a narrow crossroad.

"If you could kindly direct me downtown, then," I said, my frustration becoming great. "I have no idea where I am!" The weight of the truly curse-like events I had endured suddenly became too much to bear and I began to sob aloud, ready to give up and collapse where I stood, falling into whatever terrible destiny the streets would have for me.

He stopped and turned back, suddenly showing a hint of human empathy. "Don't cry."

The thought crossed my mind that perhaps I had died sometime during the trip from Norland, or maybe when Brantley had buried me, and now I was in Hell. If it were so, the punishment would be fitting, although the thought of enduring such a level of torment for all the rest of eternity was enough to feed my tears a little more.

He allowed me to catch up to him. "You look tired and hungry," he said.

I nodded, clasping my hands together. "I'm very tired . . . and *very* hungry."

He nodded. "Come on, then."

We approached a quaint two-story building separated into four apartments. Mr. Poe unlocked the front downstairs door.

"It's not much, but please make yourself comfortable," he said, dropping his coat onto a chair.

The apartment was small, with one attached bedroom and a fireplace. At least it was warm. "It's lovely," I said.

"It'll be the bank's in two weeks' time."

I looked down. "I'm sorry."

"I'm not. I had attempted a last-minute sale to developers, but my window of opportunity closed while I searched for an honest bidder. I refuse to do business with a shady partner, which is most likely the reason I am such a terrible businessman." He smiled faintly. "It's time to move on, just the same, even if it does mean losing this dilapidated old place."

He offered me a seat at a small table near the fireplace, where Neptune immediately made himself comfortable. Mr. Poe stirred a smoldering layer of embers before adding new logs. The logs caught quickly, and he set a kettle of water to boil from the cauldron hook.

"I'm sorry I don't have anything more substantial to offer you," he said, moving a half loaf of bread and a box of tealeaves from a cupboard. He dropped some of the tea into the kettle and set the bread on the table between us.

I tore away a piece of bread and took a massive bite. "It's very charitable for you to feed me at all. I'm sure you wouldn't believe me if I told you I've never taken charity before."

"That is not the issue at hand." He pulled Brantley's diary entries from his coat and spread them on the table. "I've been searching my mind for the connection, how I may have known your husband, but as far as I know, no connection exists beyond my own independent research on the lighthouse and his working as its keeper."

"Where could he have found your name?"

He shook his head. "Perhaps he was a fan of my work."

"Your work?" I asked, a tired, sick feeling hitting me as I suddenly noticed the numerous books lying around the apartment with Mr. Poe's name on them. "You're a writer?"

He nodded. "Still, even if he found my name and general whereabouts in a book, how did he know of my interest in the lighthouse?"

"A coincidence?"

"Impossible!"

"I don't know what else to attribute it to," I said.

He tore a piece of bread from the loaf and chewed at it thoughtfully. "Do you know the name of the person who hired him to work there?"

I shook my head.

"He spoke of no one?"

"Never."

He went to the fire to check on the kettle, then crossed to a kitchen area and removed two teacups from a cupboard. He served us each a cup then sat and stared at his cup. Finally, he took a sip and looked across the table at me. "May I ask you some questions about the lighthouse?"

I closed my eyes for a moment before turning to him with mournful eyes. "I would prefer not to talk about that place."

"I've heard too many different second-hand stories."

I shrugged and began to sip lightly at my tea.

"It's burned down twice, been blasted open by lightning, and has had to have every panel of glass in its tower replaced at least once."

I stuffed a large piece of bread in my mouth.

"It has had seven reported deaths: three by drowning, one confirmed murder, and three indisputable suicides . . . well, now, four with your husband's hanging."

I shuddered, nearly choking over my bread.

He stood abruptly and crossed to the small sitting area, where he had a desk, a bookshelf, and two large plush chairs. From one of the desk drawers, he produced several pages of notes. He set them on the table before me and sat down again.

"Why are you doing this?" I asked him.

"Just take a look at some of the accounts I've been able to collect from various locals."

I pushed away the pages, unwilling to look at them. "I have no desire to discuss other peoples' accounts of the place."

He gathered the pages, setting Brantley's diary entries to the side of the pile. He took another piece of bread and dipped it in his tea. "I'm terribly sorry.

Sometimes I let my curiosity get the better of me."

I glanced at the letter at the top of the pile, catching a couple of lines of text. My reading skills were not great by any real standards, especially in English, but for a woman they were still notable. My nanny had learned to read and write with her brothers, and she had impressed upon me from a young age the importance of understanding print. The particular letter that now fell under my glance shared several characteristics to Brantley's writings: it was composed of journal entries; it mentioned that there was something important to be found somewhere inside the lighthouse; and the words felt frantic and rushed. Most interestingly, however, was the mention of someone named De Grät, with whom I was also unfamiliar.

I pointed to the name. "Do you know this De Grät?"

He shook his head. "His name is only on these two documents, with no specific reference as to who he is. I haven't been able to find any record of him anywhere, nor can I find his affiliation with the lighthouse. I'm guessing it's a pseudonym."

Or an anagram, I thought as I studied the name more carefully. *Greta D. Greta Dahlgren, our old footman's sister's name.*

"Is something the matter?" Mr. Poe asked.

I shook my head, turning away from the text. I pushed the thought from my mind. It couldn't be that. Greta couldn't have known what had happened, and her brother had most assuredly died by Brantley's hands. There was no connection. Just the same, I moved the document in front of me for a closer look.

I read it from beginning to end. I searched for the writer's identity, but he did not appear to disclose it anywhere within the text. I looked for anything else that might explain who this mystery man was, but he might as well have been a ghost.

"Take your time. Look through them all. Maybe you'll see something I didn't," he said.

As I looked at the different documents, the question came to me: how had this man come into possession of all of these? What was his link to all of their writers? I wondered if I dare ask him, but immediately decided against it. For all I knew, *he* could be De Grät.

Neptune barked, and we both looked up as there was a knock at the door.

"Whoever could that be?" Mr. Poe muttered as he crossed to the door. "Who's there?"

"I have a message for Mr. Poe," a man's voice filtered through the door.

"Leave it on the porch," Mr. Poe replied.

"As you wish."

Mr. Poe waited a moment then peeked out. He snatched a letter from the doorstep and quickly closed the door. He opened the letter. "Hmm," he said. "I've been invited to a dinner party. Strange."

"It's strange that you've been invited to a dinner party?"

"I don't know the host," he said.

I shrugged. "Perhaps the invitation was delivered to you by mistake."

"No mistake. It says to 'admit Mr. Poe and one guest' to the formal dining hall. Not just anyone can afford to host a dinner there." An excited gleam came to his eyes. "I wonder if it has anything to do with my most recent publication. I had a feeling that would be the one to bring me some acclaim." He returned to the table. "Would you like to go to a formal dinner with me tonight, my dear?"

I glanced down at my dress, picturing the pretty, simple gown it had once been. Several days of exposure to the elements had left it unrecognizable. Did all who now saw me perceive me as a mere homeless peasant? Me, a Lady of Norland? "I don't think so, but I appreciate the invitation," I said, realizing just how ashamed I felt about my humble appearance.

"I think you would fit one of my late wife's old gowns," he said. "Would you like to take a look?"

As unusual as the circumstances behind my invitation were, the stifled socialite in me was desperate for a dinner party. And what was the alternative? Eating bread and drink tea in this dreary room?

I stood, my decision made. "If you could show me to your bath, I would like to get cleaned up before I change."

He responded with a nod and a smile. "I'll have the attendant heat some water."

I stayed beside the table, finishing my tea as he found the attendant and sent him to prepare my bath. When he returned, he held a dress in each hand. The first one was pink with burgundy sashes and tiny pearls sewn along the corset's ribs and hemlines. The second one was blue and lacy, with heavy folds of silk over the hips and rump. From Mr. Poe's fingers dangled matching bonnets and a choice of white heeled shoes.

"Will either of these do?" he asked.

I lifted the pink dress from his hand. "It's lovely."

"Good." He set down the other dress and accessories on the sofa. "You'll put it to better use than she can now."

I looked down, realizing that I was to wear his deceased wife's dress. "I'm sorry about your loss."

He nodded silently.

His attendant peeked in. "You bath will be ready shortly, Madam," he said, and then ducked back out.

"Who pays for your attendant?" I asked.

"I do," he said with the tone of a man confessing a great sin.

"If you are in such great debt, why do you continue to employ him?"

"He's an excellent handyman."

"And?"

"And I am not," he said. "This building has been a nightmare and without his help, it would have fallen down long ago."

"How reassuring," I said.

"It is reassuring."

"And you also pay him to heat your bathwater?" I asked.

"Again, I know I can trust *him* not to burn down the place."

Bathed, dressed in the formal gown and white heels, my hair combed and pulled back, I felt like a Lady for the first time in nearly half a year. I met Mr. Poe at his apartment door, and he answered wearing a very becoming suit and hat.

Mr. Poe sent for a buggy to take us across town to the inn. A young woman wearing a yellow silk dress showed us into the dining hall. The room had a long table covered with a pristine, white cloth. Beautifully polished silver sat beside expensive chinaware, complimented by centerpieces of small, intricately painted vases brimming with colorful, exotic flowers. All but three spots at the eight-seat table were filled, and two of those spots had matching nametags sitting on their plates: Poe.

We took our seats and I noticed we were the only guests with nametags. A new attendant entered, wheeling a cart loaded with wine bottles and glasses. He served us one after the next, offering us a dry but tangy red wine. I found the taste to be like none other I had tried, so I asked the man its vintage.

"I'm sorry, but I don't know," he said and moved on to fill and distribute the next set of glasses.

I took a moment to survey the group. The men all wore tasteful suits, although the man at the end of the table wore a powdered wig. He was tall, thin, and gaunt, and I suspected consumption at first. The man coughed not once, however, so I considered instead some kind of familial defect. Beside him on either side was a set of identical twins clad in matching pink dresses. Beside each of them sat two very different-looking men wearing matching suits, seemingly the twins' dates. The women wore excessive makeup and perfume, their arms and necks brimming with gold chains and pearls. I tried not to stare, although it proved a difficult feat. The woman to my left had long, frizzy hair, which she had evidently made no attempt to tame and looked strange against the refined, sea-green dress and jewel-encrusted necklace around her neck. The woman across from her was old and looked sickly, her black dress hanging awkwardly from her bony body. She had short white hair and long facial features that reminded me of old folktale witches, and she had black, beady eyes. Her expression was one of unwarranted contempt, made even worse by her unfortunate features, and I tried my best not to meet her icy glance.

Everyone turned as the gaunt man at the end of the table stood and tapped his fork against his glass. "My friends, I'm sure most of you are wondering why I have invited you all here." As he shifted, I heard a familiar noise, but I couldn't quite place it.

"Here with us tonight," he continued, sauntering down our side of the table, "is a group of people who all have something in common. Enjoy your wine, take your time, and try to come up with that that commonality is."

As he passed us, I noticed that he wore spurs, and suddenly I knew exactly who he was. I pretended to hit Mr. Poe's glass by accident, knocking it to the table. The red wine soaked into the white linen.

"Oh, dear. Look what I've done!" I said.

"Not to worry," said the gaunt man. "I'll have it cleaned and like new by tomorrow."

"Someone might think it's blood," said the old woman seated across from me.

"It looks nothing like blood," said the man closest to her, speaking in a distinguished British accent. "Blood dries an awful brown hue."

The gaunt man pulled aside his attendant. "Please bring Mr. Poe a fresh glass."

"Thank you," said Mr. Poe as the attendant walked out.

I looked around, trying to disguise my panic. I turned to Mr. Poe. "I'm afraid I'm not feeling well. Could you please walk me out?"

Mr. Poe looked annoyed, but stood and took my hand. "Please forgive the interruption. I'm just going to see the lady out." He gave me an angry look as soon as we cleared the room. "What is wrong with you?" he asked as we moved down the main hall to the front door.

I moved close and whispered into his ear: "I recognize the host's spurs. He's the man I heard in the horse stalls. He's the man who was hired to poison you."

He winced as the truth hit him, and we both began to rush for the door.

"May I help you?" the attendant asked as we reached the door.

We stopped and turned. He smiled innocently as he carried Mr. Poe's replacement wine glass.

"The lady is ill. I'm going to take her home," said Mr. Poe.

"Allow me," said the attendant. "I'm sure you'll be missed at the dinner."

Mr. Poe shook his head adamantly. "I must see her home. Please send my regards to the host."

The attendant did not try to stop us as we left, but I had the sense that someone watched us as we hurried away. Neither of us spoke again until we were in the safety of a buggy and on our way back to his apartment.

"You're certain that was the same man?" he asked

me.

I nodded. "Do you have any idea why someone would hire him to kill you?"

"The only thing I can think of would be my research," he said.

"The lighthouse?"

He nodded.

When we reached his apartment building, he locked the door and rearranged all of the furniture to block the windows. He spread the documents across the table. "Whatever it is, it has got to be here," he said.

While I began to sift through the short stack of documents, Mr. Poe pulled his most recent publication from the bookshelf. "Or the answer is in this." He sat by the fire and read, still shaking from the recent event. "I can't believe someone would want me dead over something here."

I tried to concentrate on the words in front of me, but there seemed to be nothing that hinted at anything important. Then, suddenly, it occurred to me that the hand on each document was far too similar to each of the others. There were variations, but it looked like the same person could have easily written all of them. What I noticed next, upon moving them around and finding a chronological order, was that each of them contained entries for three to five days in a different month. For example, the one I had brought from Brantley's desk had entries spanning from the first to the third of January. None of the dates on the documents overlapped. I took another look, realizing that there were no signatures or any other means of identifying their different supposed owners. Then, one final problem came to me, one I couldn't help but question aloud: "Mr. Poe, how did you come into possession of all of these?"

A look of realization came over him and he collapsed over the table in a horrified fit. "I did! I wrote them!"

"That's not possible," I said. I picked up the document I had brought with me. "Brantley wrote this! He had me bring it to you!"

He laughed incredulously as he snatched up the rest of the documents and threw them into the fire with a scowl. He tried to take mine from me as well, but I turned and ran for the door.

I looked around, realizing that Neptune was suddenly nowhere to be seen. "Neptune?" I called out.

Mr. Poe wept mournfully.

"Where's Neptune?" I asked.

"Neptune was my childhood dog. He's been dead for twenty years, sweet Neptune!"

"You're lying!"

"I knew it! I *have* finally gone mad!" he cried, grabbing the poker from the fireside.

I tried the door, but it wouldn't open. I began to cry as well, twisting and tugging on a doorknob that wouldn't turn. I looked for somewhere to run as he came at me with the poker, but there was nowhere to go. I saw a flash of light as the metal made contact with my head.

"Stop *haunting* me!" I heard him scream as my world went black.

I could hear him continue to cry out, although the rest of my senses failed me. I wanted to ask him why, after everything I had done for him, he would want to lash out in such a way, but the words wouldn't come. I tried to scream, but it was no use.

Where was I?

Chapter Fourteen

I realized that I was sinking. I felt bubbles release from my mouth. I opened my eyes, gasping in a heavy breath of water as someone grabbed my arm. I felt my body rush to the surface and my lungs go into sudden and heavy spasms as the cold ocean air hit my senses. I began to flail my limbs as I saw Brantley dragging me to dry sand. He turned me to my side and I began to sob as I heaved the water from my lungs.

"What were you thinking?" he yelled. "Or were you somnambulating again?"

I shook my head. "I've gone mad!"

"Karina?"

I flailed through the sand for only a few seconds before I realized that the near drowning had left me too weak to get up.

"Karina?"

He lifted me into his arms and carried me back to the lighthouse.

"Do you know a man named Mr. Poe?" I asked

him as he laid me on our bed.

"I don't think so," he said. "Why?"

I shook my head. "I thought I heard you say something about him in your sleep."

"He must have been part of a dream then, and nothing more."

"Oh," I said. *He had seemed so real*, I wanted to add.

"You have been so preoccupied as of late. What is it that has been haunting you, my love?"

I closed my eyes, contemplating my response. Finally, I decided to answer his question honestly: "Might it be possible that we were just a part of someone else's dream and nothing more?"

"What kind of a question is that?" he asked, probing me for some kind of added jest. When I let him know by my expression that I was serious, he looked down. "You really have gone mad."

I couldn't help but begin to weep again. "But what to do about it?"

"It's all right. I'm here," he said, placing a gentle hand on my shoulder.

I cringed back with a heavy shudder. "Don't touch me!" I shrieked before I could even think about what I was saying.

He shied away, his face trembling and his eyes tearful. "Tell me what I can do to help you, Karina! Please—I just want to help you!"

"No one can help me!"

"Don't say that!"

I tried to get out of bed, intent on running out and not stopping until I had reached the ocean and beyond, but my body was still recovering and

Brantley held me back with ease. I sobbed aloud, cursing my hellish misfortune and refusing his attempts at consoling me. How could I continue like this? I wondered how I had become so detached from reality and, more importantly, what had prompted the slip. Was any of this even real? Was Brantley dead or alive? Was I actually here, or was I somewhere else just dreaming?

"I can't stand to see you like this," Brantley said.

I didn't respond. What was there to say?

"This is all my fault. I shouldn't have brought you here," he continued. "Can you ever forgive me?"

I looked over at him, startled to see that he was crying.

"I wish you could just . . . be happy despite all of the torment I've caused you. The scandal with Greta and Dahlsen, I should never have involved you."

I nodded my appreciation, still too upset to speak.

He kissed my forehead then stood. "I should take you to see a doctor."

"But you said you couldn't leave your post."

"Your health comes first. I can't watch you suffer any longer." I let him take me back into his arms and carry me out.

"But what will we do with Neptune?"

The pained look that suddenly came to his eyes told me that he did not know who Neptune was.

"I don't have a dog?" I asked, already desperately missing the hound.

He shook his head, visibly shaken. "No, my love. There's no dog." He carried me to the rowboat, where he carefully stepped in and rested me against the seat in front of his.

Finding Poe

I closed my eyes, huddling where I sat. I felt the boat begin to stream through the choppy water as my mind worked to sift through a hurricane of nightmares and memories that twisted and tangled amongst one another in my thoughts. I thought about the dream within a dream I had experienced on the train, and I wondered if more of my life hadn't followed a similar theme. It seemed to me that at least half of what I had seen and done since moving to America had been solely within the confines of my mind. Perhaps such insanity was my personal response to the lighthouse's curse, *if* cursed it was. Either way, I had indeed gone mad.

There was no doubting that.

We took a buggy down the coast, to a property that seemed to belong more to a Gothic novel than reality. The heavy iron gates at the road bore the initials "A. A." and the two panels mirrored each other as a guard on each side pulled open his side. The property was not level, with numerous small hills covered in dried grass standing between the gate and the monstrous building. There were leafless trees all along the drive, and a few littering the hills, and I watched as a murder of ravens congregated in a couple of them. The birds screeched at one another, flying between the two trees and jumping between the branches. As if to offer aid to the ambiance, it began to rain. Lightning flashed. Thunder crackled into the distance.

"I don't like this place," I whispered.

"But you do know it's for the best?" Brantley asked.

I nodded meekly, although I had begun to have

terrible doubts. "Perhaps we might try something else first?" I asked.

"What else is there to try?"

I thought about it for a moment, but I was not able to think of anything.

"I'm sure the treatment will be quick," he said, and I swallowed hard.

The building looked far too old to belong to New England, with its high stone walls, thick ivy, and rusty iron bars. Grim-faced stone gargoyles crouched over the tall eaves, staring down at us as we exited the buggy and ascended the front steps.

The door was locked, so Brantley used the heavy knocker. It was only a moment later when a woman wearing a pressed, white nurse's hat opened the latch to a small peek-hole.

"May I help you?" the woman asked.

"I wish to seek treatment for my wife," Brantley said

The door opened and the nurse allowed us into a spacious entry hall. There were chairs on both sides and a set of closed double doors on the far wall.

"Please wait here," said the nurse, and we sat as she crossed to the double doors, unlocked them, and hurried out, locking the doors behind her.

We sat in silence while we waited for the woman to return. There were no clocks within view, so I could not say for sure how long we waited, but I would estimate that we sat there for at least twenty or thirty minutes, speaking not one word to each other all the while.

When the nurse returned, she had two men clad in white coats with her. "These men will show you into the ward and check you in. Are you wearing any jewelry?"

"Just my wedding band."

"Best leave that with your husband." She snatched the ring from my finger and handed it to Brantley. "If you'll come with me, Mr. Reynolds, I have a document for you to sign." She gestured to the two men.

The men each took one of my arms and coerced me toward the door. A sudden panic took over me. "Brantley! I don't want to go!"

"I'll send for you soon, my love," he said as the men dragged me, screaming and flailing, through the double doors.

Had Brantley known how different the building would be on the other side of the double doors, I'm certain he would have not left me there . . . but how could he have known? Even I had not suspected that it could possibly have been that bad, and what my senses took in stunned and alarmed me at once. What first struck me was the smell. How one set of doors could hide a reek so horrid I could not tell, but as soon as we reached the other side, it hit me. It was putrid but meaty with a distinct hint of urine. Although I could not see the direct source to the stench, it was obviously the collective smell of the committed.

What struck me next was the lack of color. Everything there seemed to be either black, white, or a shade of gray: the walls and ceiling were covered in a dingy whitewash; the molding was dark, nearly black, and the floor was a staggered combination of white and gray tiles. Where there was not an attendant to watch a lamp, all was dark. From the darkness came the moans and screams of the insane, the defiant, and the forgotten.

The two attendants took me into a room, where they expected me to remove my clothing.

"Absolutely not!" I cried.

"You have no choice," said one of them as he pulled at my bodice.

"We can't have you bringing in lice or disease," said the other.

I screamed and fought in vain as the men took away my clothes and shamelessly, thoroughly inspected my body, then took turns violating me with the thermometer until the nurse entered the room, at which time they declared me physically healthy and free of vermin. The nurse handed me undergarments and an overused frock. The frock was stained, made of a thin material, and not in the least bit becoming. When I told the nurse it was unfit attire for a Lady of Norland, she told me they had the Queen of England there as well, and she found the frock to be quite suitable. With nothing else to wear, I donned the thin, itchy frock and followed the nurse back down the hall in my bare feet.

"This is the day room," she said, pulling a key ring from her dress pocket and unlocking the door. "This is where you get to go during the day if you behave."

There were about a dozen women in the room, in ages ranging from young adult to elderly. While most looked lucid and active, a few of the women looked detached. One seemed oblivious that she sat in her own waste. All of the patients wore matching gray frocks.

A lamp burned from an adjoining room, where another aid sat looking bored. He peeked through his office door as we entered.

"Newcomer?" he asked.

She nodded as he unlocked the secondary door and waved us through.

"These are the sleeping quarters," the nurse said as we entered the hall. Most of the doors were closed, the rooms dark, a few of them imprisoning the most unruly of patients.

"This is where you'll spend your days if you don't behave," said the nurse, looking me in the eyes to make sure I understood. "You want to make sure that doesn't happen."

I nodded. The hall was chilly with a draft pushing through the outside winter air from some unknown source, but I trembled far more violently than the cold warranted. I could not believe I would be staying in such a place, that I would be living, sleeping, and eating here until the doctors deemed me well enough to return home. I wondered how long it would take, noting that some of the women looked as though they had been here for some while.

"You're just in time for supper," said the nurse as she led me back into the day room. "It should be anytime now."

I shuddered as the attendant locked the door behind us.

"Have a seat," said the nurse as I surveyed the grim lot once more. She joined the attendant in the next room, spoke with him for a moment, then crossed the day room and exited into the main hall.

I sat down on a hard, wooden chair that had been

set aside on its own. I watched the other patients watch me, wondering what they were wondering. I dared not look any of them in the eyes, the animals some of them appeared to be, and I found myself staring at the floor in fear of making any immediate enemies.

I jumped as a young woman about my age sat down beside me.

"Scared?" she asked.

I shrugged.

"It's only natural," she said.

I turned to her, surprised to find sympathetic eyes amidst her wild hair and ragged frock. "I don't want to be here," I whispered.

"I know," she said. She paused for a moment then asked, "What's your name?"

"Karina."

"Glad to meet you, Karina. I'm Leonora."

I nodded my recognition.

"What brings you here?" she asked.

I took a deep breath, hoping the woman might leave me alone without another word.

"I'll start," she said, immediately moving into her unsolicited story: "My husband and I had secured passage on a boat across the sea, but a thief attacked us on our way to the port. I survived the attack; he did not. I knew I needed to continue with the journey as planned, but I could not leave my deceased husband behind. It had been his dream to see America, and dead or alive, he was going to realize it. I knew that no captain would allow a corpse to travel across the ocean on his vessel, so I arranged for the body to be set in a crate filled with salt. I had the crate put in the cargo hold, then took my room, watching through porthole, silently weeping as the ship went to sail and I saw my homeland for what I knew would be the last time.

"I tried to sleep, but although the bed was plush and the pillows feathery soft, my thoughts held upon the long, pine box that lay so cold and alone amongst the cargo. I alone knew what was in there; or, rather, *who* was in there. I thought about what he might have felt down there . . . and what he might have said if he still had the means to speak. I couldn't help but ponder the terrible and frightening question: *Could the dead speak?*

"I became so upset over my thoughts of the body having to lie there alone like that, I went down to the cargo hold in the middle of the night to mourn over the box. Finding the hold unbearably cold, I leaned against the box and tucked my legs against my body. I sat there for some time before I heard the first signs of the body shifting within the thick salt grains. I felt my senses go acute, the movement within the box prompting within me the terrible fear that perhaps he had not been dead after all. Could I possibly have ordered the man packed in salt whilst he was still alive? The question ate at me, despite all logical reason telling me that there had absolutely been no mistake.

"But then I heard yet another shift in the salt followed by what was undeniably a moan, and I turned to the box with a cry of my own. 'Can you hear me?' I asked it and fell into sobs when I heard nothing else.

"Meanwhile, one of the ship's hands had

discovered me there, but instead of confronting me, he went straight to the captain. Both men rushed down to investigate, only to find me attempting to pry open the box with my bare fingers. They stopped me of course, neither willing to let loose whatever smells of decay that lay contained therein. I tried to convince them to help me open it, just to ensure all was well with its contents, but they banned me from the room and told me I and the box would have to vacate the ship at the next closest dock.

"Of course, by the time we arrived to the nearest dock, my box and I had created enough of a stir to prompt a call to the constable and a ride here. Can you believe it?" she asked.

I shrugged, still unwilling to speak to the woman.

"But it was worth it," she said, her eyes glossing over with the threat of tears. "My beloved Kenneth was buried on American soil. It may not have been the new beginning we had planned on, but we both made it here—and here we'll both stay."

I glanced up at her. "You don't seem at all mad to me."

"Sanity has nothing to do with being here," she said, pointing to the attendant's office with one hand and placing her forefinger over her lips with the other.

We both quietly watched as the attendant locked the office and disappeared down the adjoining hall.

"What's he doing?" I whispered.

This time, it was she who did not respond. Instead, she listened, her body language advising me to do the same. After only a minute or so, I began to hear the pained cries echoing from one of the rooms.

"What's he doing?" I tried again.

"Punishing them," she whispered back.

"What is he *doing* to them?"

"You don't want to know."

I turned to her. "Do you know?"

Leonora nodded. "You don't want to know."

The woman down the hall gave a blood-curdling shriek. I tried to run to the door to see what I might do, but Leonora stopped me.

"But what—" I began.

She placed a finger over my lips, shaking her head and leading me back to my seat.

"Why is he hurting her?" I whispered.

"Because he can," Leonora said.

We both pretended not to notice when the attendant returned to his post. He surveyed the room, then sat down with a deck of cards and began playing Solitaire. Moments later, the nurse entered, pushing a cart loaded with food trays. She distributed them quickly, and I eagerly accepted mine, only to find a stale piece of bread and a slimy slice of pork scrapple for my meal, seemingly to be eaten without any kind of utensil. At first, I could only register the possibility that the nurse was playing a trick on the newcomer, and I even laughed. When no one laughed with me, I realized that this nearly rotten, hardly edible concoction actually was meant to be my supper.

I stared down at the tray on my lap, trying to discern by smell what it actually contained, but that only put my already upset stomach into fits. I tried to suppress it, but I could not hold back a sickening series of gags and wretches. To my fortune, my stomach was empty and had nothing to vomit, but that did not keep my body from making the attempt.

I watched the other women eat, using their hands in place of spoons, surprised by the ease in which they accepted their mystery food. I set my tray on the floor at my side, unwilling to try it. The nurse took notice and left her observation post to confront me.

"Eat your supper," she said.

I crossed my arms. "I will eat when you present me with something edible."

She set the tray back onto my lap. "This is what you're getting and this is what you'll eat."

I tilted my knees and allowed the tray to fall to the ground. The awful mass splattered in all directions, flinging grease onto my frock and the nurse's apron.

The nurse put her hands to her hips, her angry glare reaching across the room to the attendant sitting in the office. He moved to join her.

"She's refusing her supper," said the nurse.

The attendant snatched my wrist, twisting it in a way that sent me forward and onto my knees. He pressed my face into the fallen contents as I screamed and flailed.

"Eat your supper!" he screamed.

I tried to fight the man off, but he was strong and I was weak. I held my lips tightly shut as he mashed my face even harder into the slimy, mushy mass of meat.

"You'll lick the floor clean or you'll get your own private room in the back," said the nurse.

"Just do it," I heard Leonora whisper.

"Please just do it," I heard another woman's voice add.

My heart heavy and my throat tight, I began to eat

the food from the grimy floor. It tasted every bit as awful as it looked and smelled, but I forced down every bite, my will breaking a little more with each one. I felt the sting of tears threaten to add to my captors' satisfaction, and I disposed of them as discreetly as I could as I wiped away the beads of sweat that had begun to develop across my face. The food had no distinct flavor, although I could discern a slice of carrot here and a morsel of meat there. Overall, it was the texture that was the worst of it, being slimy, crunchy, and meaty depending upon the bite, and that combined with the smell of it was nearly enough to make me vomit it all back up. Somehow, I finished the meal, and the nurse allowed me to get away with wiping the remnants from the floor with the front of my frock.

Appeased, the nurse and her attendant returned to their station and locked themselves behind their screen door. I stayed on the floor, too humiliated to move. I could hear the other women eating all around me, some of them whispering amongst one another, when Leonora leaned over my shoulder.

"Keep your chin up. They're going to get what's coming to them very, very soon," she whispered.

I turned to her, only to find her chewing a mouthful of her scrapple. She gave me a wink as she took another bite, feigning to enjoy the decadent morsel of a fine cut.

I wiped my face with my frock, watching the nurse and attendant stare back at me from the safety of their locked office. They too had words to whisper back and forth between them. I tried to discern what they might be saying, both of them continuing to stare, when Leonora leaned into my ear again.

"You got lucky," she said. "I've seen girls get put in the back over much less."

"But why?" I asked.

"I guess we've all just been here too long," she said.

"How long have you been here?"

"A *long* time," she said.

"How much longer until you get to leave?" I asked.

She scoffed. "You don't leave."

"But they can't just keep us all here indefinitely!"

"Shh! Don't worry about that. Just keep your head down for another day or so. Can you do that?" she whispered.

I nodded. I wanted to ask her what that meant, but she walked off to chat with another patient across the room. I sat in silence, listening to the mumbles all around me, unable to filter one voice from the rest. I couldn't help but assume that most of them were whispering about me, given the looks I seemed to get from all directions, but I couldn't have begun to guess what they were saying. Still, something told me I had an ally in Leonora, so I kept my head down and waited for whatever was to come "in another day or so."

Even with my head down, I bore witness to such chilling examples of human degradation that I have been left without words to describe the crimes. The attendants abused the women in isolation every chance they got, and those of us in the common area suffered random "treatments" that were as torturous as they were varied. Those who fought back found themselves locked alone in one of the back rooms.

Leonora told me that the walls and floors of the back rooms were stained with human waste and blood, that the one time she went back there, she came out with a case of dysentery so severe she thought she might die. She told me about the maddening isolation, the sounds that would come from the neighboring rooms, and the terrible things the attendants would do to her when the nurse was gone.

"They killed a woman once," she said.

"What happened?" I asked.

"They were trying to get her into the hydropathy room and she didn't want to go. I don't know what exactly they did to her, but we all heard the screams. She must have continued to fight because it only seemed to get worse . . . and then everything went quiet. None of the staff said anything when they returned, and none of us asked, but Annabel saw all of the blood."

"Annabel?"

Leonora nodded. "They made her clean up the mess. She's been in isolation ever since."

Chapter Fifteen

During my short stay at the asylum, I learned that most of the women there were no more insane than I was. Many had been brought in by their husbands for refusing to submit to their every demand, while a few simply had no place else to go. A few of the women there were indeed mad; I had the chance to meet one of them before the attendants took her back to isolation. Her name was Virginia, and she approached me on my second morning there.

I had found the routine simple, and yet the structure was difficult to accept. The nurse and two attendants entered the common sleeping room at dawn, at which time we had five minutes to wipe the sleep from our eyes and make ourselves presentable. The room smelled of soiled linen. The women, a mob of greasy hair and sweaty frocks, got in line to use the restroom. They ate their breakfast in the common sitting area, where most of them would spend the rest of the day. A privileged few would leave to work at a ranch nearby, and here and there, a woman would tearfully leave or enter isolation. Supper came early in the evening, and they ordered us to retire to the floor for the night immediately after dusk.

I had just finished a breakfast of nauseatingly greasy scrambled eggs and dry toast when Virginia sat down beside me.

"Do you know your purpose in this world?" she asked me.

I shrugged, unprepared for such a random question.

"Everyone should know their purpose," she said.

"Do you know yours?" I asked her.

She nodded adamantly. "My purpose is to make sure *everyone else* knows their purpose."

"Then do you know my purpose?" I asked.

"Oh, yes!" she said then jumped from her seat and began to fidget all around me. She clapped her hands. "Yes, yes, yes!"

I tried to contain her, but she seemed possessed by something far too excited and amused to be able to pay any real attention to me. She did turn back to me as she carried on, and she even spoke to me when it suited her, asking indiscriminate questions such as, "Have you ever pondered what it would feel like to be beheaded?"

That particular question was not among the strangest, but her insistence to carry on about every detail of her imaginings definitely struck me as most strange. "First off, I would hope the blade was filed to the perfect edge, so it would not take multiple blows to sever my head from my body," she began. "Did you know that a bad blade can make multiple blows *quite* necessary?"

I shrugged indifferently.

"Even with a good blade, could you imagine the pain involved if the executioner didn't get it right upon the first hack?" she asked. "The shock of such a blow to the back of the neck, only to find it not quite lethal. What torture!"

I shuddered.

"I should think it very surreal, when one finally did lose one's head," she continued. "I'm sure the pain would still be there, quite all the way through from the back of the neck to the front of the throat, but the pain would be nothing compared to the distress of being a severed head in a basket. Wouldn't you think?"

I shrugged, turning my back to her.

"You wouldn't be able to scream because your throat would be cut in half," she continued. "All you would be able to do would be to look around in that little basket and wait for God's judgment. What do you think it would be like in that basket?"

I ignored her.

"I think it would be Hell in a hand-basket!" she said with a shriek and a laugh.

I crossed the room to the barred window, hoping she would take the hint, but she followed me. I stared blankly at the surrounding fields of dry grass and rotting oaks, and she pretended to do the same.

"I think drowning would be the worst way to die," she said.

I felt a heavy jolt in my chest at the sound of her words, but I continued to stare silently out the window.

"Think of it: the flood of liquid rushing into your

lungs, the gasping, the choking, the thrashing about, desperate for air, feeling your body slowly slipping away. How terrifying would that be?" she asked.

I closed my eyes, laboring to hold my tongue. I could not say for sure why such simple *words* might affect me so profoundly, but they evoked such a level of terror in me that it was all I could do to pretend I hadn't heard any of what she had said. I could sense that she was working purposefully to provoke me, and I was determined not to give in to her obvious attempts at intimidating me.

She moved her lips to my ear and whispered softly, "*Maelström!*"

"How do you know that word?" I asked, swallowing against the sudden tightness in my throat.

She laughed loudly. "*Maelström!*" she yelled. "The ship is capsizing!" She took me by the shoulders and attempted to take me to the ground, and I threw her off with a horrified screech. She came at me again and the attendant rushed out from behind his cage and tackled her.

I watched as she fell into strange fits of alternating laughter and cries, tears streaming down her face, a surreal smile stretching her lips ear to ear. The man subdued her with a sudden and jarring twist to her arm behind her back, and she collapsed with a pained cry. I watched—we all watched—as he dragged her to the door to the isolation rooms, holding her with one hand as he used the other to unlock it, then closed the door behind them as soon as they cleared the threshold.

Her screams were especially unnerving, the tones and lengths some of them took being as such that one would think they would have been reserved for Hell alone. We all heard her though, and we all knew better than to tell the nurse when she came back from her rounds at the adjacent wards. Leonora had come to me as soon as she was certain the plans were in place. "No matter what happens, keep your calm," she said.

I pried for more information, but she would say no more.

Supper came. It was comprised of mashed potatoes and some kind of ground meat, but I could not identify it. Some kind of vegetable was also in the mix, as I saw bits of green here and there, but it too was unidentifiable. I ate what I could, having learned my lesson the hard way that one did not refuse the meals provided here unless one was a glutton for abuse. Such types existed, but I was not among them.

Shortly after we had all finished our meals, one of the women began to act out. She sprang about the room like a wild Ourang-Outang, grunting and gesticulating provocatively at all who would look. Of course, the nurse and attendant stormed out of their observation room to deal with the woman. She made their intervention difficult, moving all about the room and inviting other patients to do the same. Just as the attendant was able to apprehend her, the most peculiar thing happened. He passed out. Then the nurse ran to assist, only to collapse unconscious herself.

At first, I could only look on with confusion and uncertainty as Leonora and a few other organizers went into action. They dragged the nurse and her attendant into the isolation hall, where they locked each in a different room. They then released those who had already been locked away and directed everyone to the door to the main hall. I joined the others at the door, and we waited eagerly as Leonora unlocked the door and thrust it open.

As the first of our group burst through, Leonora called to them, "To the executive dining hall!" She and a few others directed us not toward the asylum's front doors, but down the hall the opposite way. They led us into a room with a long dining table set with crystal goblets, polished silverware, and fine chinaware. We sat as another group filed in from the men's ward, effectively filling every seat.

"Tonight we feast!" Leonora exclaimed, and we all cheered.

We cheered even louder as the nurses and attendants were paraded around us. They now wore hospital frocks and their hands were bound with torn strips of bedding. The larger of the male patients helped to direct the small group out of the room, and then we heard the men and women of the staff emit cries and screams that were already all too familiar to us. Only this time, it was a sound of justice. This time, the sound did not evoke feelings of nausea and horror, but of satisfaction and contempt. Leonora spat on the floor and we all followed her lead.

A man wearing an ill-fitted doctor's coat strutted in. "Thank you for joining me tonight, ladies and gentlemen," he said over the low din of voices. "None of this would have been possible without all of you."

We all cheered.

"After careful planning and organized execution, we have oppressed the oppressors and reclaimed our freedom by force!" he continued, and we all continued to cheer. He sat at the head of the table, opposite Leonora.

He waited for our cheers to abate then added, "We survived their ice-water baths and their hot water therapies!"

"Yes!" the patients cried, a few of them with heavy shudders.

"We survived their tooth-decaying, body-rotting mercury treatments!" he added.

"We did!" replied those sickly pale and missing multiple teeth.

"We survived the tranquilizer chair and the spinner!" he continued.

Everyone cheered. I looked around, unable to mask my confusion.

Leonora leaned in close and murmured into my ear. "The tranquilizer chair is one of the contraptions they have in the isolation area. They strap you in so you cannot move, then they put a box over your head so you cannot see or hear anything. They leave you there until your world becomes that box, so that even your cries for release become meaningless. Then, finally, after you've soiled yourself too many times to count and you've bruised your wrists and ankles from the struggle—after you've given up all hope that the world continues to exist, then they take away the box and remove the straps and send you back to the sitting room to show off your newfound sanity."

"How terrible!" I said.

She shrugged, moving in even closer. "That's

nothing compared to the spinner."

"What's the spinner?"

"They strap you into a chair that goes round and round and spin you in circles until everything becomes a blur. But they don't stop there. They keep it going until up becomes down and you cannot help but vomit all over yourself. They say the vomiting is cleansing, but we all know better. They do it to keep you sick, to make you feel sorry for yourself so they can move you on to the bleeding treatments. They say all these treatments get the blood going in the right direction. Well, I say the best treatment of all is freedom. I think we've finally made our breakthrough!"

Two women in stolen nurse's uniforms entered carrying bottles of absinthe. The women stopped by each of us, pouring a generous serving of the bright green spirit. I had consumed absinthe before, but with sugar, which turns the drink a lighter, hazy color and cuts the bitterness. I watched as everyone around me began to take puckered sips. I followed suit, as not to stand out. My lips tingled as a peculiar sense of warmth and well-being washed through me.

"Now that we have overturned the hierarchy here, it is time we reassign all of the duties to be performed at this lovely establishment," said the man in the doctor's coat. "Who else would like to be a doctor?"

Nearly everyone raised a hand.

He pointed to another man seated beside him. "You can be my assistant." He pointed to Leonora. "You get to be the head doctor of the women's ward."

Leonora nodded and smiled.

"The rest of you get to be nurses and attendants.

We'll distribute uniforms after drinks," said the mad doctor.

A young man sitting near the center of the table jumped to his feet and began to cluck like a chicken. He circled the table, pretending to peck, randomly stealing sips of absinthe from others' glasses between searching for crumbs of food to eat off the floor. I watched others' reactions to gauge my own response, surprised to find that no one seemed at all troubled by the man's peculiar behavior.

"I have carefully considered the severity of our patients, and I believe I have come up with some excellent strategies we might use in our approach to treating them," said the man clad as a doctor. He finished his glass and invited the rest of us to do the same.

The second glass of absinthe did not taste nearly as terrible as the first, but by then all of my senses had grown a little fuzzy. The group began to get loud, with everyone trying to speak over everyone else in their intoxicated excitement. Someone came in with a stack of white, pressed coats and aprons and began to hand them out. Another patient had discovered the real doctors' and nurses' effects, and distributed them equally amongst us. I felt a sobering shock of realization when I found another woman's wedding band in the palm of my hand. I looked at my own bare finger, feeling the empty spot, and I could not bear to replace it with a symbol of someone else's union. I set it on the table in front of me, catching Leonora's attention.

"You don't want it?" she asked.

"I have my own at home," I said.

She grabbed it and gleefully put it on her finger. "Perfect fit!" she exclaimed, even though it moved about like a bangle.

The absinthe hit me suddenly, and I looked around with new eyes at the surreal scene that surrounded me. On both sides, there was the discomfort of women stuffed in ill-fitted aprons and madmen in doctor's coats and half-buttoned attendant's shirts. They laughed and joked without a care, which troubled me greatly. Despite my intoxication, my body felt rigid and nervous. I sweated profusely and fought a light queasiness. I closed my eyes as the room began to spin.

Leonora shamelessly changed into her doctor's clothing where she sat, the shirt and pants ballooning over her relatively small frame. She donned her white coat, grabbed a nearby young man from his seat, and the two began to dance a crude waltz. "Do you hear the music?" she asked.

I could not hear it. I had grown far too concerned with all of the candles lighting the room. There were three candelabra on the table and two or three sconces to each wall. Their flames moved in a way that nearly entranced me, stretching and writhing as if aware of their movements. The candle fire from the sconce on the wall directly across from me seemed to reach for the wall behind it. Curiously, no one else seemed to notice. It teased me, singeing the wall before suddenly backing off, then going back to blacken a little more.

"Are you all right?" Leonora asked me.

I shook my head. "I think I need some fresh air."

She jingled a key ring. "Let's go get some then."

Chapter Sixteen

The rain and lightning had abated, so that now a thin fog crept over the peaks of the dead lawn, slowly moving and swirling around the other greenery and dissipating against the stone walls. It gave the landscape an ethereal feel and I nearly questioned whether I was really there. Had it not been for the wintry air and the discomfort it caused me, I would have assumed I had fallen into another one of my fitful dreams. Every sensation was too acute, though, and my reaction to the green alcohol was too great for this to be yet another trick. Of course, my frame of mind was not at its most lucid, so I could only feign to say what was real and what was not.

I turned to ask Leonora if she knew how to get back to the coast, only to find she had left me. The realization that I was alone seemed to add to the surrounding chill, and I became aware of the breeze as it stirred up the fog. I looked back at the building, unsure how to feel as I noticed ravaging flames dancing behind the blackening windows. Smoke began to seep out from the roof in thick, heavy clouds, and then all at once the roof collapsed. I rushed off, lest the entire building collapse with me in its path of destruction.

The iron gate clamored in the wind, somehow threatening in itself, but I sprinted toward it without disinclination. I caught it mid-swing, threw it open, and hurried out onto the private road. I turned back around just in time to see the building fall into a mass of fire and rubble. I heard screams, but I dared not go back for anyone. Instead, I began the long walk back to the main road. The nearby ravens called amongst one another with great agitation, and I could nearly make out words between them. They could see what was coming. They could see the shadows that followed as I fled the scene. They screamed and cackled as they took flight over me just to add to the torment, and in quick and reckless move, I picked up a stone from my feet and hurled it at the ugly, black mass. I saw one of the birds go down with a screech, its body flailing.

I walked up to it, immediately sorry for what I had done, watching in horror as it flapped its wings and kicked its legs. And then it was dead. A haze fell over its eyes and its beak fell open, the change from living creature to carcass being shockingly visible and profound. It brought a sudden ache to my chest, that I had been the cause. I cursed whatever had possessed me to throw the rock, wishing I could take back what was done.

The ravens knew not my remorse, however, and when the murder realized what had happened, it began to attack. I covered my head as the birds dove down at me in waves, and I ran as quickly as I could in search of cover. I flinched with a cry as one of the birds bit me in the face, then another in the back of the neck. I tried to bat them away as they neared, but there were too many of them. With nowhere else to go, I dove into a dense patch of thicket and, while the birds continued to attack, they no longer had the advantage of being able to dive down into me. I waved madly all around me, thorns tearing at my arms and face, when I realized that the birds were no longer there.

Carefully, tentatively, I crawled out from my hiding spot and rose to my feet. I looked around, and despite the heavy fog that now obscured everything, I could not recognize my surroundings. No longer was I on the private road leading to the asylum. Instead, I now stood somewhere altogether unfamiliar. There was the glow of lit lamps on both sides of the road, and as I moved to find a closer look at one of them, I saw that I now walked along closed storefronts. I flinched as I heard a raven caw from some unseen place; however, no creature came.

Another sound caught my attention, and I turned to search for the source as it grew louder. The sound was rhythmic and deep, and it only took a moment for me to realize that what I was listening to was a drum. It grew even closer, and soon I could see silhouettes approaching through the fog. The drum echoed through the street, pulsing through my body, forcing my heart to pound in synchronicity. I stepped back as the parade approached, and my breath escaped me as I watched the line of men dressed in doctor's coats lead a handful of tarred and feathered men and women by ropes about their necks. I silently watched them pass, and after only a minute or two, the sound of the drum waned into the distance with them.

I stepped into the light of the nearest lamp, barely able to distinguish the flame through the fog. My heart still pounded, the beat of the drum returning in my head. Flashes of the gruesome parade invaded my mind's eye. A second sound began to overlap the first, only this sound was faint and high-pitched. It came with every beat, though, and after a minute it was all I could hear. It grew louder as it moved closer, and soon I saw the gleam of a small bouncing marble as it approached. Curious, I tried to catch it as it passed, but missed. I followed it as it stopped bounding and fell into a roll.

Finally, I caught it and raised it with my trembling hand for a closer look. With a gasp, I watched the glass eye look back at me. I dropped it, surprised when it shattered at my feet. I looked up, realizing that I stood before a slightly ajar door. Tempted to escape from the cold, eerie street, I entered the building.

I walked down a long hallway with pitch for walls and a stone floor. Red candles dripped from black sconces, their flames dancing ominously as I passed them. There were no doors as far as I could see, save the one at the end of the hall. It was open about a foot's width, letting in light from the connecting room, and I could hear a waltz coming from inside. Familiar with the song, I hurried to the door to discover the source.

I stepped inside to find myself in a strangely

familiar masquerade ball. I glanced down at my attire, embarrassed that I did not have a gown and mask. I thought to leave, turning with a start as someone behind me tapped my shoulder.

"May I have this dance?" the man asked in a familiar voice as he bowed. He wore a black and red suit, black gloves, and a large black hat. His mask resembled a skull, with an appearance so real that it gave me chills.

I gave him a nod and a curtsey, and the two of us began to move along with the rest of the guests. He led gracefully, gliding my body across the floor with perfect form. I held my frame in line with his, my head tilted in confident repose.

"Do you know the lord of this estate?" my dancing partner asked me, his hand brushing my hip as we turned and spun.

"I do not," I answered.

"I was not invited either," he said.

A strange feeling came over me. "I must go," I said, then politely curtseyed and hurried off.

To my surprise, my dancing partner followed right behind me. He stopped me at the door. "Are you sure you don't want to stay for tonight's festivities?"

I considered his question. "Festivities?"

He nodded. "It's almost time." He produced a second mask from his coat. It was a woman's face, oddly similar to my features. He handed it to me.

I took a closer look at the mask, surprised by how realistic it actually was. It looked just like me, down to every feature. The sight of it was unsettling. I turned back to the man, unsure of what I should do next.

"Aren't you going to see how it looks?" he asked me, pointing to a mirror on a nearby wall.

I raised the mask over my face as I crossed to the mirror, fighting to steady my shaky breath. I looked at my reflection through the eyeholes, my hands trembling at the surreal sight. I saw my dancing partner come up behind me, and I flinched as he placed a hand on my left shoulder.

"It's time to unmask!" he said, removing his.

To my horror, the face beneath the mask looked no different, the man's gaunt, skeletal features otherworldly and menacing. His features seemed set in a permanent smile, and he watched me through hollow eye sockets. I stood, frozen in my terror as the people all around us began to fall to the floor, dropping their masks, gasping and grabbing at their throats. I pushed past the man, knowing he had come for me, and I stumbled through the threshold as I reached the door that led back to the hall.

I ran through as a cold wind rushed past me and blew out the candles along the walls. Unable to see, my heart racing, I kept my hand along the wall and continued as quickly as I could.

"Where are you going?" I heard the Masked Death call from behind me.

"Leave me alone!" I yelled back, struggling to keep my pace.

I heard his footsteps slowly gaining on mine, the exit nowhere in sight. I hadn't remembered it to be so long before and in my anticipation of the door ahead, I reached desperately in front of me. I approached no door, however, and as the footsteps behind me drew closer, I felt my panic escalate.

I screamed when the floor dropped beneath me and I fell into a free-fall through the darkness. My limbs flailed as I reached for something, anything that might break my fall. Landing hard on my back, my breath escaping me with the impact. I lay gasping, struggling to catch my breath, still unable to see anything, when I heard another man began to wail.

"Get off me!" he cried.

I heard the squeal of a rat.

I cried out as I finally regained my breath. "Hello?" I called to the man.

"What do *you* want?" he replied angrily.

"Can you tell me where we are?"

He burst into an incredulous laugh. "Where are we? Where *are* we?"

"Do you know?" I asked.

"Could you untie me?" he asked. "I'm strapped down and the rats are eating my fingers."

I strained to see as I could hear footsteps from somewhere not too far off.

"Here he comes!" said the man between laughs. Another rat squealed. "Ha!"

I scrambled to my feet and began to move, stumbling over the rocky ground. Tears stung my eyes as I stared into the darkness, waving my arms madly in front of me in search of the nearest wall. The footsteps grew louder the closer they moved, until each step sounded like a thunderous crash. I hit a cool, rocky wall, and I realized that I was in some kind of cavern.

"Hey, I'm over here!" yelled the strapped-down man.

I followed the wall, ignoring him, my hands

searching for a door. The sound of the man's yells echoed through the chamber, reverberating against the footsteps that moved ever closer. I tripped over a jagged rock, flying forward and skinning my hands and knees as I skidded to the ground. The wounds stung and a part of me wanted to give up, but I jumped back to my feet and resumed my search of the wall.

The man shrieked, "Get off me!" and I cringed as I heard another rat squeal.

I found a corner and turned it, realizing from the light up ahead that I had entered a long tunnel.

"Where are you going?" the Masked Death's voice echoed from some unknown place within the cavern.

I darted down the tunnel despite the rocky surface, knowing that I ran for my life. I watched as the light slowly grew. It illuminated the tunnel's mouth, shining like a beacon that would steer me to safety. As I reached it, however, a new sense of confusion and horror came over me.

I entered a brightly lit room consisting only of bookshelves and a writing desk. A few empty bottles littered the floor. Sitting at the desk was a man scribbling madly onto a sheet of paper. He grumbled, took a mouthful of rum straight from the bottle, refilled his fountain pen, and continued.

"Hello?" I asked meekly.

Either he couldn't hear me or he chose to ignore me, as he did not respond.

I stepped closer, the floorboards creaking beneath my bare feet, but still he refused to acknowledge my presence. "Hello?" I tried again.

He hastily grabbed a handkerchief and pulled it to

his mouth as a heaving cough jerked his entire body. I stopped where I stood when he set the handkerchief to the side and I saw that he had coughed up a mass of dark, clotted blood. With another grumble, he grabbed the rum and swallowed a sizeable gulp.

"I'm sorry, but I don't know how I got here," I said.

The man continued to write.

"Can you tell me where I am?" I asked. "I need to get back to my husband, back to the lighthouse."

He stopped and turned to me, and I recognized him immediately as Mr. Poe. His eyelids were droopy and his movements exaggerated in his intoxication. "The lighthouse?"

I nodded. "Do you know how I can get back there?"

He scoffed.

"I'm sorry to disturb you," I said.

He took another swig of rum. "Of course you're not! You know, I'm writing this as quickly as I can!" He turned back to his writing. He snatched the handkerchief just as a heavy coughing fit racked his body, revealing more blood as he set it back aside.

"You're ill."

He scoffed again.

I took another step toward him. "If I might suggest—"

"You may wait your turn!" he snapped.

I went silent for a few seconds, taken aback. Finally, I said, "I'm just trying to help."

He went completely still, seemingly jarred by my words. With a labored breath, he set down his pen, stood from his desk, and turned back to me. "As gracious as I am for all of the 'help' I've received over these dark years, please understand this." He paused, looking me intently in the eyes. "I am but one man, and I have sacrificed everything for you people. I have summoned up and given into my greatest fears for you, and I have done it gladly, for I know the importance of our work."

I shook my head. "You're not making any sense."

"I'm tired and I'm empty," he continued before finishing the bottle of rum.

"I think you're drunk, sir."

"Ha!" he exclaimed, turning to sweep the pen and sheets of paper that sat on the desk. "I need some fresh air!" he said, then staggered to the door, stumbling straight through me.

I took a moment to process what had just happened. *Was the man a ghost?* Was this another dream? Would I ever know normalcy again? I jumped at the sound of the door slamming shut behind him. I happened to catch a glimpse of one of the pages on the floor, stunned to find that Mr. Poe's writing was about the lighthouse.

I hurried to the door and opened it, feeling dizzy as I saw that the tunnel had been replaced by a familiar Baltimore street. It was eerily desolate. I saw Mr. Poe hurry away, knocking into lampposts and walls in his drunken fog, and I ran to follow. "Sir!"

"Not right now!" he cried. "I need to clear my head!"

"I just want to ask you something!" I called to him.

"*Not right now!*"

I watched, unsure what to do as I watched the man

collapse with a pained gasp. He tried to get up, only to fall back. I looked down both sides of the street, seeing no one as I ran to his side. "Hello?" I yelled. "Somebody?"

Another man turned a corner, spotting the fallen Mr. Poe.

"Please help him!" I cried.

I cursed after the man as he ran off, only to find that he had gone to retrieve help. Mr. Poe stumbled back to his feet, alarmed when the man and two others approached him.

"Are you all right, sir?"

"They're driving me mad!" Mr. Poe cried.

"Who's driving you mad?"

Mr. Poe cried aloud. "I'm sure you wouldn't understand!"

They loaded Mr. Poe into a buggy. I hurried in behind them, startled to find that my body passed through that of another man there.

"Am I a ghost?" I questioned aloud, startled by the possible revelation.

Mr. Poe turned to me.

"Am I a ghost?" I asked him.

A pained smile moved across his face. "You don't know?" He laughed.

"What? Tell me please!"

"No ghost could haunt me the way you people have," he said. His eyes rolled back and one of the men began to slap his cheeks. Mr. Poe looked ahead once more with a startled gasp.

"What's happening to him?" one of the other men asked.

The man closest to Mr. Poe tried to address him.

"Sir, can you speak to us?"

Mr. Poe ignored them, instead continuing to focus on me. "A ghost!" he said with a strained laugh, shaking his head. "Oh, my head!"

"Sir?"

"Then I'm not a ghost?" I asked.

"Far from it," said Mr. Poe. He cried out, his body seizing.

"He's delirious," said another one of the men.

"Sir?" the other tried again.

"Mr. Poe, what's happening to you?" I asked.

"I don't know," he cried.

By the time we got to the nearest hospital, Mr. Poe was moaning and writhing and unwilling even to speak to me. He began to call out random names, yelling nonsensical musings at the ceiling.

I followed him into a room, where a doctor began to assess his condition. "Can you hear me?" he asked Mr. Poe.

Mr. Poe shook his head back and forth, but not in response to the doctor. His movements were pained and seemingly beyond his control. His face was locked in a tight grimace and both of his hands closed into tight fists. "Please, oh please, oh please!" he cried. He gasped then cried out again.

The room began to grow dark.

"I think we're losing him," I could hear the doctor say.

"God help my soul!" I heard Mr. Poe gasp with his dying breath as he and everyone else in the room began to fade away.

Chapter Seventeen

Suddenly, I was at sea, standing just outside the captain's quarters among a small crew on an unfamiliar vessel. We fought heavy winds and powerful waves.

"*Moskoe-ström!*" one of the men yelled.

I turned to see that we headed directly for a giant whirlpool. The ship sped as it fell into the vortex, and I watched as the crew worked frantically to direct it free. There was no use, though, and moments later, the *Maelström* swallowed us all.

THE END.

OTHER BOOKS BY LEIGH M. LANE

George Irwin remembers a time before the Big Climate Change, back when the airlines were still in business, back when people still drove their own cars and the bulk of humanity had not yet been driven underground. Back when all people were still people despite their eye color or which class they were born into. . . .

The world has changed much over his lifetime, but George still believes in the American Dream. However, when an alleged terrorist act lands his wife in the hospital, George stumbles upon a secret that could mean the end of all civilization.

AFTERMATH
Beyond World-Mart

From the author of *World-Mart* and *Finding Poe*

LEIGH M. LANE

When all seems lost, when all the world has crumbled away, what will rise in its place?

In this highly anticipated conclusion to the World-Mart trilogy, George once again travels beyond the district in search of possible surviving family. What he finds along the way, however, changes everything he thought he'd known about the world—and the end of the world—as he knows it.

Travel alongside George, back through the deviant shanty-towns and beyond, to a place he'd nearly forgotten—and to another he never could have imagined existed.

The world of corporate greed runs rampant after the government collapses, leaving police, fire, and social services in the hands of the wealthy. Debtor prisons for the lower and middle classes overflow and quarantine camps have filled to capacity, turning the streets into a personal battleground for terrorists fighting against a world headed toward ruin as resources run dry and civilization becomes ruled by The Private Sector.

"In the tradition of *1984*, Leigh M. Lane delivers a terrifying vision of the future--a horrific future that may not be so distant after all...." -Lisa Mannetti, Stoker Award-Winning author of *The Gentling Box* and *Deathwatch*

LEIGH M. LANE

Myths

of

Gods

*A Tale of What Always Has Been
and Never Will Be*

After stumbling upon the creation of existence and life, God attempts to resolve petty religious conflicts by coming to the people in the form of five prophets. Instead of setting the people straight, however, the five—the individual embodiments of mind, matter, time, life and death—inadvertently set off a chain of events that will leave time, space, and humanity forever changed.

Take a critical look at religion through an infant God's eyes in this dark science fantasy allegory that spans from the Big Bang to present day.

ABOUT THE AUTHOR

Leigh M. Lane has been writing for over twenty years. She has ten published novels and twelve published short stories divided among different genre-specific pseudonyms. She is married to editor Thomas B. Lane, Jr. and currently resides in the dusty outskirts of Sin City.

For more information, including upcoming works and anthology contributions, visit her website at http://www.cerebralwriter.com.